THE LANGUAGE OF LIGHT

A statewide anthology of Minnesota student writing from the 1982-83 COMPAS Writers & Artists-in-the-Schools program.

Poetry Editor: Michael Moos

Fiction Editor: Patricia Weaver Francisco

Design: Sharon Anderson/Joseph Heffron

Illustration: Mary Bergherr

Copyright © 1983 by COMPAS Writers & Artists-in-the-Schools. All rights reserved. No part of this book may be reprinted or reproduced without the prior permission of COMPAS.

COMPAS
Landmark Center, Room 308
75 W. Fifth St.
St. Paul, MN 55102
Molly LaBerge, Executive Director

Typesetting: Peregrine Cold Type, St. Paul

The title for this book is taken from a poem by Kristine Maschka of Mankato East Junior High School, Mankato.

ACKNOWLEDGEMENT

COMPAS, the largest community art agency in Minnesota, produces and sponsors a variety of multi-disciplinary art activities for people of all ages and abilities. Each year more than 160,000 Minnesotans enjoy and participate in COMPAS art activities in community centers, churches, businesses and schools.

The COMPAS Writers & Artists-in-the-Schools program places professional writers and artists in Minnesota public and private schools for week long residencies in poetry, playwrighting, fiction, visual art, music or theatre.

The COMPAS Writers & Artists-in-the-Schools program is made possible by a grant provided by the Minnesota State Arts Board through an appropriation by the Minnesota State Legislature and in part by a grant by the National Endowment for the Arts. Additional support is provided by the Blandin Foundation, for writing residencies in northern Minnesota, the Jerome Foundation, for residencies conducted by fiction writers, the Otto Bremer Foundation, for residencies in designated communities, the Jostens Foundation and school districts. COMPAS, a member agency of the United Arts Fund, is recipient of a McKnight Foundation award administered by the Minnesota State Arts Board.

COMPAS also wishes to acknowledge 3M, First Banks and the Saint Paul Companies whose generous contributions to the United Arts Fund have helped publish the 1983 COMPAS Writers & Artists-in-the-Schools anthology.

A NOTE TO TEACHERS:

The Writers & Artists-in-the-Schools anthology celebrates the work done by the students who participated in the 1982-83 program. The book is also intended to aid teachers in the teaching of creative writing. With this in mind, *The Language of Light* has been divided into thematic sections to allow teachers to find easily a number of pieces on a particular topic or idea.

If there is a COMPAS writer in residence at your school, he or she can demonstrate how the anthology might be used in teaching. A good way to prepare students for a COMPAS residency would be to read some of the poems in the anthology to students. Knowing students their own age have written published poems will both spark their interest and inspire confidence in their own writing. All writers use other writers as models, and students need to know this. *The Language of Light* is an excellent tool to start this process.

TABLE OF CONTENTS

I. HORSES, SWANS, PUMPKINS AND TUMBLEWEED   19

The Divine of a Shiny Horse	Mikey Ysker	20
The Eternity of the Clam	Kathy Barrows	21
Afraid of Water	Christine Jones	22
"Listen to the rain dance"	Meri Herrmann	23
(*Zusamen*) Together	Bruce Messelt	24
Swan	Julie Haar	25
Yellow	Michael Wackerfuss	26
"In the bottom of the cool, green valley"	Lisa Peterson	27
An Elephant Never Forgets	Amy Stacy	28
"An angel's heart is made of the silence of a cloud"	Steven Robberstad	29
White Poppy	LeAnn Phipps	29
The Grasshopper In The Jar	Bridget Swanson	30
The Worlds In The Dog	Keith Swanson	32
"I like to sit at the pond"	Jennifer Anderson	32
"Bob looked as if he was attacked by a wild bear"	Ryan Danielson	33
An Abandoned Ship	Nicole Forde	34
Of Course	Becky Birch	35
The Beasty	David Nolby	36
I Am A Pumpkin	Christine Ramaley	40
My Rabbit's Death	Amy Millner	41
Not a Perfect Tree	Dave Edinger	41
Tumbleweed	Margaret Marrier	42

II. THE SPIRIT OF THIS PLACE 45

The spirit of this place	Brian Mosbey	46
"A desert in Africa"	David Mills	47
Stars 1	Jennifer Schultz	48
"School is a puppet show."	Melissa Buben	49
How To Remember	Lara Tebelius	50
Old Chicken Coop	Andrea Bruchu	51
"I have learned to go back to the house on the corner"	Ken Gust	52
The Sun	Risa Weidman	53
Home	Bob Dailey	54
"This is a picture that I draw of myself"	Jayme Zachman	55
The Barn	Craig Solem	56
Connection	Jenny Woods	58
On the Farm	Brent Kubat	59
Grand Canyon	Sheri Byrne	59
My Old Truck	Tim Kurowski	60
One Lonely Satellite	Rich Holmes	61
How to Grow a Sun	Peggy Renneberg	62
This Is My Real Life	Tracey White	64
The City Boston	Jennifer Baltes	65
London	Molly J. Harten	66
Train City	Dan Fritsche	68
I Am Healed	Bobbie Jo Huss	69
Welcome to Herbert's Happy Hip Hamburger Haven	Robert Goldberg	70
The Forest	Andy Flint	71

"When you stepped into Louis Prescott's room"	Keiko Sugisaka	72
"In the sea"	Nick Kuklok	73
An Exercise in Digression	Fred Fremgen	74
I Am The Universe	Nathan O'Connor	75
Ivoryous	Steve Ochry	76

III. ART AND THE HIDDEN DOOR 77

Self Portrait	Caroline Thomson	78
A Hidden Door	Julie Athman	79
"I have a book inside of me"	Connie Sutherland	80
My Left Hand's Image	Alisa Richetti	81
What if it Went on Like This for Weeks?	Denise Holmes	82
The Sandpiper's Song	Karen Cooper	84
A Time of Death	Russell Boebert	85
Sunrise	Brad Schwartz	87
School's Out	Scott Dolan	88
Moon Books	Aaron Leichter	90
"As we sit here the day flies by"	Ann Bauer	91
Ending	Su Price	92
(haiku)	Scot Ninnemann	92
"I am a horse without a rider"	Nina Barjesteh	93
"My ears heard the untuned guitar"	Cindy Falley	94

"As I walked down the street"	Maria Edington	96
"The memories of the flag"	Bobby Foster	98
"Death is like a test. . ."	Jeff Ukestad	98
"If a tuba was made out of moonlight"	Rachel Reksten	99
When Will I Die. . .	Tana Stromseth	100
"The sounds of waves crashing to the shore"	Peggy Grant	102
"This is for those who wake"	Karen Schillewaert	103
Frustrations	Tracy Siegfried	104
(haiku)	Tami Volk	104
"The ground was parched"	Julie Haurykiewicz	105
The Poem Nobody Likes	Greg Johnson	106
Death	Jeremy Olson	107
"Sawing cat in half guts"	Mary Sharratt	108
Green	Julie Krueger	109

IV. MY FAMILY IS A BOX OF CRAYONS 113

"My family is a box of crayons"	Stephen Marsh	114
"The lemonade is getting watery"	Kris Hansen	115
Dusty TV	Kari Frechette	116
A Daisy	Shane Johnson	118
"Me and my grandmother would always make"	Helena Kriel	119

Waxing	Steve Worner	120
Older Brother	Julie Vennewitz	122
My Father	Susan Adams	123
Uncle Joel	John Cooper	124
Moving	Kerry Dammen	125
Hip Boots	Al Hegquist	127
Someone's Watching	Tim Lander	129
Dad	Michele Narlock	133
In Diapers	Christine Strander	134
"I am the stage"	Becky Leder	135
The Sun	Stuart Meyer	136
Cream Separator	Peter Jacobs	138
"Fists swinging"	Brad Benike	139
Childhood	Robbie Reed	140
The Sidekick	Troy Renslow	141

V. THE PICNIC OF DREAMS 143

Invite a Lion to Dinner	Amy Lee	144
The Lonely Times	Sharon Bachman	145
Getting Fat	Mark Swenson	146
"I am a star that hit a window"	Craig Uhl	147
My Imagination	Jenny Belisle	148
"The salty sea air blended in"	Jodi Schmieg	149
The Woodsman	Denise Berg	150
No. II	Paul Christensen	152

Waiting For Spring	Matt Shuey	153
"Let me never become a Rock"	Steve Schwanz	153
"The ground is hard and cracked."	Cameron Black	154
The Life Of A Dream	Carrie Saba	155
The Flame	Jason Walton	156
A Strange Sweater	Val Leske	157
"A kite is like a bird"	Josh Squires	158
Cold Winds and Dark Nights	Andrew Bonnette	160
"down go they"	Joseph Hsieh	161
"In my dream I dreamed that"	Jennie Sullivan	162
I Am A Cloud	Marcy Olson	163
Tomorrow's Door	Tom Gibbons	164
My Dream	Liz Bamberg	165
Laura	Susan Shea	166
My Wondrous Find	Lynne Zeige	168
The Reflection	Jeff Maas	169
The Girlish Tree	Lisa Erickson	170
"Where is my secret?"	Tony Thaler	171
The Language of Light	Kristin Maschka	172

A NOTE FROM THE EDITORS

We are writing, our hands fly across the page, we move without hesitation, our minds turn to water, spill words, our pens fly across the page. We ask very little—clean white paper, a pen with ink, time and a place. We let our wrists ache, we pay no heed, our pens fly across the page, we are rushing. We write, we get it down, we get it all down, we do not stop to think about what we are missing, if we write fast enough we will say the one thing that has been left unsaid. It is day, it is light, we are writing. We listen to words rise up behind our eyes, chime, it is right, this word rings, sings. We never stop, this is food enough, the world goes by, we pull it, pull it in.

In classrooms all across Minnesota, students are writing. Some stare off, suddenly not in a classroom at all but wandering in a forest, imagining a deer with strange green eyes and a little girl lost in a cave. Others dive into the page, their eyes only inches from the paper, in furious pursuit of memory. They do not worry their words. They write with the energy and ease that comes from being allowed to tell their own stories. They are delighted with their words and it shows.

Explore the pages of this book—moments and whole universes vie for your attention. Let this book take you back to a time when new worlds appeared before you as you lay flat on your back and named the clouds. When your age allowed anything to be possible.

What is most striking to me about the stories in this collection is how much these writers know—of paradox, fear, the beauty in a grandfather's gnarled hand, the precise sound of wind. Flannery O'Conner has said:"Anyone who has survived to the age of 18 has enough material to last them the rest of their lives." Indeed these stories show us that childhood is not as innocent a place as adults wish to make it. But they also attest to what it is— a time of clear individual vision, vivid imagination, heart and a remarkable perceptiveness.

Sometimes I think that we who work with students in the COMPAS Writers-in-the-Schools program ask the impossible. We ask students to invent, visualize and share deep feelings all in the space of one short classroom hour. But they have risen delightfully to the occasion. These writers are as at home with metaphor as with their own names. Inside every story about a land or people they have never known are feelings which are uniquely their own. There is evidence in them of much love for the world and a critical eye cast toward indifference and injustice. This bodes well for the future.

The stories in this book are not meant to lay silent inside these covers. Like living things, they contain the energy that was used to create them. Respond to these stories with your own. Let them call up memories, dreams, old regrets and the characters of life. Read them, read them aloud, read them again.

Patricia Weaver Francisco, Fiction Editor

I'm in a classroom opening a book of poems, letting out my first lesson of the day. From an adjoining room, beyond the accordian wall, a familiar music turns my head. I know the piece, but the name won't come. An eighth grade girl wearing Nikes cracks her knuckles and mumbles, "The William Tell Overture." A constellation of images surface from my past . . .

I'm up north in a cabin on Eagle Lake. Thunder. Lightning. Summer rain through the dark. My grandmother, mother and father play gin rummy at the kitchen table. I'm a little boy wearing a Smokey The Bear T-shirt. I'm listening to The Lone Ranger on the radio. I keep thinking about the snapping turtle my father caught by chance just before the storm, how it fought to stay alive, its beautiful Rorschach under-shell fading like a memory . . .

I tell my students maybe there's a poem among these details recalled from childhood. How I feel about my family, distances, the taking of a life, atmospheric and emotional weathers, the passage of time. Maybe a poem can be a kind of time machine? I think of Darwin on the Galapagos. Connections. I remember The Lone Ranger's voice, how I imagined his eyes, his mask. Is a poem a kind of mask? Maybe I'm like the radio's antennae when I make a poem, receiving signals through the air.

Maybe this is how a poem evolves, sometimes. Perhaps within these images lives a potential harmony, a longing for order. When we feel in sync with the universe, when the gods are with us—is that the moment of a poem's conception? When we feel like a sliver of peace in a discordant world. When we stop trying to orchestrate the world, stop waiting for it to become perfect. When we feel accepted and accept what comes to us. Is the writing process a metaphor for the way we live? From a boy in the back of the room: "All that reminds me of the time I..." I focus on my students' hands. They're writing.

This book is filled with poems by Minnesota students who have interacted with a variety of writers giving of themselves in similar, yet distinct ways. One of the pleasures for me in selecting these poems has been to become reacquainted with the generous and compassionate spirits of the COMPAS poets. As I read through this book I can sense their individual presences; yet their fingerprints are not to be found. These are real poems. There are no easy formulas here. These poems are fueled by honest, human voices taking their first flights into the familiar and the unknown.

Many of these poems let us participate in the writer's most personal world, his/her daily life. They speak of emotional struggle, dreams and lost jobs. They speak of wilting roses, human survival, worn-out plaid shirts, the need for work and companionship. The playful dialogue of the seasons is here and sorrow and joy and small town grocery stores and gray barns and hope. Our cities, highways, attics, backyard gardens, suburbs, farms, and Minnesota families are here. The desire to know and praise one's grandparents seems a recurrent theme. These poems will make you laugh; they'll bring tears.

Another triumph of these young writers is that in taking risks with their everyday language and their imaginations, they have transcended their autobiographical landscapes, allowing us to read our own stories in theirs. I think of a line written by Thomas Transtromer: "Every person is a half open door leading to a room for everyone." These are poems of childhood, adolescence and young adulthood. But their concerns and loves belong to all of us.

Michael Moos, Poetry Editor

THE LANGUAGE OF LIGHT

HORSES, SWANS, PUMPKINS AND TUMBLEWEED

I

THE DIVINE OF A SHINY HORSE

I am a horse, a four legged mammal
with hair so thin and silky within
divine. And a tail so perfect and
straight down with a curl in place
all bundled up so light. With a
dance so glory and neck so high and
departs so quick through the air like
silk is thread through a silver
pointed pin. Its body so straight
as a pickled pear and teeth so shiny
and glow. Its saddle so smooth like
leather and a color of brown like
a piece of whole wheat bread.

Mikey Ysker/grade 4
Westwood Elementary School, Blaine

THE ETERNITY OF THE CLAM

Inside the world of a clam,
you are in darkness. It is a
quiet place, you wait for the
glorious sunrays to come when
the clam opens. You have time
to think your problems out.
There is a myth in this place
that says there is a monstrous
sized pearl and if you find
it everyone can escape the
loneliness of the clam forever.
No one works here—they just
search for the pearl. They
don't try to make do with
what they have, they just
dream.

Kathy Barrows/grade 10
Woodbury Senior High School, Woodbury

AFRAID OF WATER

I'm afraid of water like a duck's afraid of turtles
waiting patiently for the right moment.
Seeing his chance, sneaking up quietly,
ever so quietly and attacking,
dragging the poor duck down deep into the water.
The duck trying her hardest to reach the top,
not able to hold her breath any longer.

I've been afraid of water ever since I saw the turtle.
I'm afraid he's lurking in the weeds,
afraid any moment
he'll come out of hiding.

Christine Jones/grade 8
Pine River High School, Pine River

Listen to the rain dance on
my soft glittery mud puddle.
Listen to the horse trot
or drums beat
or thunder crack
or wind   sneak up behind
or clear crystals dance
through the air
or pearls drop through
the lightning
on the cool ground.
Open the door to the
pouring shattering
glass in the
cold still air.
Listen. Listen.

Meri Herrmann/grade 4
John F. Kennedy Elementary, Hastings

ZUSAMEN

Alle die Tiere sind schon
   hier,
Jeden neben einander.
Allein Sie sind Nur Sport fur
   Jager, und Fleisch fur Man
   und Kinder.
Aber Zusamen machen Sie ein
   Gesicht von Angst, dass Nemand
   Kann eben sehen.
Was bedeuttet dieses fur Alle
   uns hier?
Wen nur Mann kann' versteh'.

TOGETHER

All of the animals are already
   here,
Each one next to the other
Alone they are only game for
   hunters, and meat for
   man and children.
But together they make a face
   of fear that no one
   can even see.
What does this mean for all
   of us here?
If only man could know.

Bruce Messelt/grade 11
Central High School, Duluth

SWAN

Inside a swan I see
Beauty that overwhelms me,
Love that comforts me.
But a swan inside is
like no other kind of bird.
Let someone else be a cockatoo.
But I will be a swan.

A swan may be beautiful
inside but it may also carry
deep sorrow and grief. Like when
a boy throws a stone
at the swan from the side
of the creek bank.

A swan is most beautiful
inside. Perhaps it hides its
sorrow with beauty.

Julie Haar/grade 6
Tanglen Elementary School, Hopkins

YELLOW

In the morning
  the tulips
    come into
      bloom
  by the
    sound
      of
    the
  tuba. In
the evening
  the
sunflowers
  fly
across my
    lawn
    and
  the daisies
  roll in the
     sky.
  In the night
  the moon
  shines so
bright the dandelions
turn cartwheels on
    my lawn.

Michael Wackerfuss/grade 3
Central Park Elementary School, Roseville

In the bottom of the cool, green valley, the early morning dew is still on the grass. Mares placidly graze, occasionally swatting a fly with their long tails. Their young foals play tag on the side of a hill, the warm sun making their soft coats shine like polished brass.

One colt is bolder than the rest—he races around the valley, hurdling fallen trees and challenging the other colts to fight. His nostrils flare in the morning air; he goes unchallenged. Tiny hoofbeats echo over the hills as he charges up to his mother. The echoes fade as he noses up to her warm milk. Now that his feet are still, the crickets' trilling becomes pleasantly audible, punctuated by the call of a killdeer and the cry of a crow.

Suddenly, the mares' heads shoot up, the grass is forgotten. The sound of a truck is heard, coughing and sputtering in its effort to climb the steep hill. The foals run to their mothers, who form a circle around their vulnerable offspring. A gunshot is heard, followed by a series of gleeful shouts. The truck tops the hill, and begins a not too smooth descent. The mares and foals charge away from the vehicle; several guns fire; two mares scream, then fall; their legs are still moving, churning the air, but they go nowhere. More shots are fired, more horses fall, but the survivors press on, trailed by the deadly truck. The bold colt is tired, he stumbles, and falls, too exhausted to rise. The truck passes him, an empty beer can bounces out, the colt goes unnoticed. He lives.

Lisa Peterson/grade 10
Battle Lake High School, Battle Lake

AN ELEPHANT NEVER FORGETS

An
elephant
never
forgets
its
memory
is
like
a
fish
that swims
to
every
port
of
the
imagination

Amy Stacy/grade 5
Chaska Elementary School, Chaska

An angel's heart is made of the silence of a cloud
and the heart of a bird is made of a music box
that makes one sound.

*Steven Robberstad/grade 4
Pine Hill Elementary, Cottage Grove*

WHITE POPPY

White flower in the park . . .
Bloom every day . . . One of the
flowers died in the park,
it was a white poppy.

White flower in the park dies when winter
comes.

Then white flower blooms every
summer.

*LeAnn Phipps/grade 5
Savage Elementary School, Burnsville*

THE GRASSHOPPER IN THE JAR

After one last jump, the green grasshopper is wishing so badly to get out of the jar. He wonders, will I ever get out?

He tries for another jump, grasping the great big jar. Grimly he misses and falls endlessly to the bottom.

The jar is filled with gleaming green leaves and glowing grass, but is ever so lonely.

Looking out of the jar, I see only an empty world—space—with no answer to give me and no meaning at all.

I wonder, will I ever get out of this jar?

Bridget Swanson/grade 8
Shakopee Junior High School, Shakopee

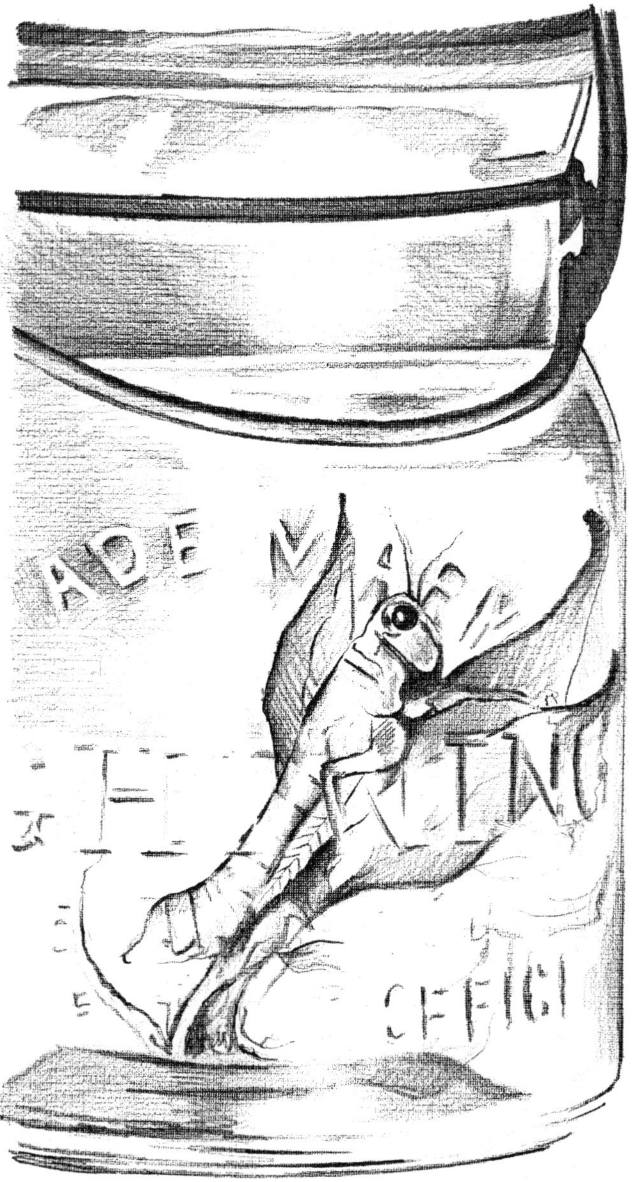

THE WORLDS IN THE DOG

Inside my dog I found a world of lush, green gardens
And in this world I found a river of sweet, cold water
In this river I found an endless plain and from
This plain I entered a space of nothing, no time,
No place, just empty space.

Keith Swanson/grade 7
Fridley Junior High School, Fridley

I like to sit at the pond,
watching silence ripple the water.
I look at my reflection
and see salmon jumping onto the shore.
The salmon are silent like rocks.
Some rocks make noise,
but only when you strike them.

Jennifer Anderson/grade 4
Riverview Elementary School, Grand Rapids

Bob looked as if he was attacked by a wild bear. His dark hair was like barbed wire and he had one sleeve off. Bob also talked like a bear. He liked to fight. Before I knew it he was in a fight with my friend and the other sleeve was off. Then Bob moved to Canada. He wrote to the class once a week. Here's what he wrote: "I hear wolves. They sould like the crowd when the Twins play." He also wrote about the huge green fish on his line. "But I think the graceful eagle got it." Then the teacher told us that we had to write back. Here's what my friend wrote: "Dear Barbed wire head, I will send it back." And he wrote back. "I hope you step in a trap and lose your big toe. I'm glad I don't have to hear you and I don't have to see you or smell you and see your banana-like nose." Then, somehow, they got to be good friends, somehow.

Ryan Danielson/grade 4
Cohasset Elementary School, Cohasset

AN ABANDONED SHIP

It's a creaky ship
and it's painted black and white.
It's on a farm where an
abandoned farmhouse stands.
Below that big old brown house
there's a river, and there were
rattlesnakes down by the river
slithering over baby toys,
and in that river were eels and things
like that, and there were
tentacles on the land.
I think it was an unknown animal.
What do you think it was?

Nicole Forde/grade 4
Riverside Elementary School, Moorhead

OF COURSE

Of course
the waves wash sea shells to shore
and let them awaken again
so, it is for sure.
Of course
the finger has been pricked by a needle
and the blood slowly creeped out.
Of course
the tail of a pheasant is frosted
and covered with black pearls.
Of course
the bud of a flower opens in spring
and lets the beauty show
of course
love is the signal.

Becky Birch/grade 7
Coon Rapids Junior High School, Coon Rapids

THE BEASTY

"Ow!" Ritchie yipped, his dusty brown hair hanging in his face. Ritchie had just painfully awakened from his afternoon beauty rest. "Ow!" he repeated, "What the . . . ?" Ritchie peered out from his layers of blankets and sheets to his long, bony, and quite ugly feet, only to find his pet scorpion gnawing on his toes.

"You blasted jerk!" he complained, and swatted it with his hand. He sat up, rubbed his sleepy, irritated eyes and plumped out of bed.

"Here, fishy fishy, come get your din din." Ritchie tossed a few northerns into his tank and watched as his piranhas devoured them, then whistled Dixie up the stairs.

"Ritchie Allen Palonzo!" Ritchie's peace was broken. "You come up here this instant!"

Ritchie regretfully forced his feeble legs up the few remaining steps and planted himself before his mother's feet.

"Well?" His mother spoke in a loud, clear, masculine voice. One could understand why he'd be afraid. His mother, or "Mommy" as he called her, stood about 6'4" and was built like an ox. "Well?!" she continued, "Are you two ever going to learn!?"

"Well, I was going to . . ."

"Going to what? Ever since you and Kevin brought that stupid BEASTY home, nothing's ever been the same around here! Those killings all over the place and everything!"

Ritchie's mom was talking about the BEASTY that he and Kevin kept. Ritchie had found it back in the woods one day and brought it home to the shack in the back.

"But . . . b . . . but we . . . ," Ritchie stuttered.

"But nothing!" snapped back his mother. "You two get rid of the BEASTY or I will! Do you understand me?" She tugged on Ritchie's ear. "DO YOU UNDERSTAND ME?!"

"Yes . . . ow . . . yes," Ritchie whimpered, and stumbled back down to his room and locked the door. Ritchie sat on his bed and thought a moment, then grabbed for the phone to call Kevin. Kevin, Ritchie's neighbor, looked just as dumb, if not dumber, than Ritchie, although he was a few inches taller.

"Hello?" Kevin answered the phone, politely.

"Yeah, Kev? This is Rich. Guess what, we've gotta get rid of the BEASTY."

"Wha—?!" Kevin sounded confused. "Why?"

"If we don't, my mom will, and you know it! I'll meet you in the backyard at, hmm, say 9:00, that'll give us an hour so we can meditate first."

"Click-click . . . buzz," came the reply on the other end.

"Boy!" Ritchie said, perturbed, "He must be ticked! He didn't even say goodbye!"

Time passed quickly for Ritchie, before he realized it, it was time to regrettably dispose of their very own BEASTY. No one had ever seen the BEASTY, that is, no one but Ritchie and Kevin. But no one cared.

"Pssst!" a signal came from the bushes. Ritchie stopped on the patio.

"Huh?"

"Pssst, I'm over here!" The whisper seemed faint.

"Well what'a ya . . ."

"Shhhh!!"

Ritchie toned his voice down. "What ya doing in the bushes?"

"Duck down, boy an' shut-up!" Kevin ordered seriously. "Da Commies are out, and I think dere after da BEASTY." Kevin was always playing *Kevin Versus Commie!*, as he called it. "Day got ammo, too!"

"Yeah?" Ritchie played along with the game. "What'a say we make a dart for the shack, okay Kev?"

"Y . . . Yeah," Kevin seemed in thought. "Yeah, but we gotta be quiet, dem commies are all over da place!"

"Sheesh!" Ritchie mumbled, staring a moment across the horizon. He ran down low and on his tip toes, just to please Kevin. A sudden 'twap' sound rang through the air. Kevin skimmed across the ground to where Ritchie was hanging by his feet, dangling.

"Ritchie!" Kevin whined, "That's my commie trap, an' you ain't no commie, so now that's one extra commie that's gonna get away!"

"Ah, would you shut-up about the commies and get me outa this contraption!"

Kevin hoisted himself up on the low branch where he had previously tied the rope, and immediately began gnawing on it.

"Must you do that?"

"How else do you expect me to get you down," argued Kevin. "I left my jack-knife at home."

"Well, you'll never . . ." Ritchie's words were broken by the thud of his head impacting the ground. "Ooooo!" he groaned, "Do you sharpen your teeth every morning or what?"

Kevin shrugged.

"What's gotten inta ya anyway, Kev? You sure have been acting strange lately."

"I guess I'm just nervous. I mean all the killins an' everything. I mean why do they think the BEASTY is the one who done it. Now we gotta get rid of him."

"Well all the victims have gashes and claw marks on them. You know that, Kev, what else could've done it?"

"Yeah," Kevin agreed reluctantly, handing Ritchie a handful of dried up raisins, and they snacked on the way to the shack.

By now, darkness was upon them. The moon shone brightly through the broken panes of the dilapidated crude windows and cast wild shadows amongst them. The door creaked wide.

"BEASTY?" Ritchie called. No answer.

"He must be out again," Kevin suggested, "we may as well go back inside."

"No way. We're going to have to wait for him again, and you are too! I remember last time I let you go, you never came back, when the BEASTY came and I had to feed him all by myself. No way! We're staying!"

Kevin sat down on an old crate that lay in the corner across from Ritchie and pouted. He pulled out a pacifier and began chewing on it.

A half hour passed. Both Kevin and Ritchie were getting restless.

"I never had to wait this long for him before." Ritchie seemed shocked.

"Well." Kevin jumped. By now the moonlight had penetrated all corners of the shack. "I've really gotta be going, Ritchie."

"Just a little bit longer, Kev."

"No, Ritchie, I gotta go, now!"

"Settle down, Kev! I'm sure he'll be here any minute."

Kevin was in hysterics. He shook all over. He turned and stared Ritchie in the eyes. Tears flooded down his cheeks. He glanced out the window to the glistening moon and then back at Ritchie. "Rich!!" he finally screamed and collapsed on the floor underneath the table.

"Kev!" Ritchie answered, concerned. "You're not afraid of the BEASTY, are you?"

Kevin peered out from underneath the table, his face covered with coarse gray hair stained with blood. "NO!" he panted. Black claws extended from his fingernails. "I am the BEASTY!"

David Nolby/grade 11
Fridley Senior High School, Fridley

I AM A PUMPKIN

One day the rain came down hard on my head. I was all wet when the rain stopped. Then I saw a really big rainbow. Just then, as I was looking at the rainbow something broke my vine; it picked me up. Then it carried me to this building and set me down on the table. Then something cut my head, this silver thing scooped out all of my insides. Then something cut out my eyes and nose and mouth and put a candle in me and put me outside. Then a boy came up to the door. I thought he looked very cute. I tried really hard to put a great big smile on my face. He picked me up and carried me home. He put me in lots and lots and lots of cold ice so I would stay fresh. He took out the hot candle and threw it away. Then I fell asleep. The next day he put one of my seeds in the garden.

Christine Ramaley/grade 3
Washington Elementary School, South St. Paul

MY RABBIT'S DEATH

My rabbit's name was Top Rank.
His black and white fur was as soft as a mink.
I will never forget him—he was tame as a cat.
He was killed by a car zooming by.
Every second hurt me, not him.
If he was alive, I would feed
and pet him in his cage.
But now he is as dead as an old dinosaur.
I remember he was like a flower
as a baby.
Each night I ask God to tell
my rabbit, I love him as much as
a mouse loves yellow cheddar cheese.

Amy Jo Millner/grade 3
Washington Elementary School, Detroit Lakes

NOT A PERFECT TREE

Oh yes, the tree needs water,
Yes, the trunk is crooked,
Yes, it is leaning eastward,
Yes, the backside is bare,
No, the angel on top is not unhappy.

Dave Edinger/grade 12
Mariner High School, White Bear Lake

TUMBLEWEED

Skeleton
of a life
wrenched
from the ground
and forced
to travel
as a disciple
of the wind.
Following
at his
every whim
on its
self-destructive
journey
across
nowhere
to
nowhere.
Reaching down
I
gently
pick it up
playing God
over
the insignificant,
and throw it
in the fire,
releasing it
from
dizzying chains
and freeing
a soul
to pursue
natural rest.

As
the grateful
spirit
rises
in smoke,
I am
compelled
to think
of my own
life,
destiny,
and purpose
if any.

Margaret Marrier/grade 12
Park Senior High School, Cottage Grove

THE SPIRIT OF THIS PLACE

II

THE SPIRIT OF THIS PLACE

The spirit of this place
Is an icy planet,
The wind never ceasing,
The temperature never rising.

The spirit of this place
Is the middle of a dust bowl,
The sand swirling frantically,
The sun baking the land by day.

The spirit of this place
Is an old ghost town.
The people have gone—
The bomb has come.

Brian Mosbey/grade 8
Oltman Junior High, St. Paul Park

A desert in Africa is like a hot sauna. It's
like being in a pot of boiling water on the stove.
Triangles are all over the ground having a war
with sidewinding squares and the munching circles
in the superstrong animal war. 3,500 blue cakes are hitting
each of the ovals in the face. The flying rectangles are dropping
live cactus plants from the greenish-purple sky
on the silver strips. There are too many green cases
of blue mice. There are too few black stars from
the moon. Friend, let's fly to Africa and get some
triangles, sidewinding squares, munching circles, blue cakes,
ovals and flying rectangles, and bring them to our class.

David Mills/grade 5
West Elementary School, Worthington

STARS 1	*STARS* 2	*SALT STARS*
Do	Are	How
stars	stars	did
shout	diamonds?	stars
out	Are	get
like	they	salt?
a	salt?	Did
spider	Are	the
plant	they	salt
or	rabbit	flow
like	popcorn?	with
fireworks?		the
		breeze?
		How
		did
		salt
		get
		up
		there?

Jennifer Schultz/grade 4
Belle Plaine Elementary School, Belle Plaine

School is a puppet show.
God is pulling our strings.
The puppets that are best
are the teachers at their desks.
Kids are the puppets
who get floppier every day.
I am one of the better puppets, a ballerina
who can dance the day away.
There's a boy, a goody-goody tin soldier
who will march all day
while the others are running,
dancing and goofing around.
There are a few pinocchios whose noses grow.
Too many clowns there are,
so the principal cuts their strings,
and you hear the cries of clowns
outside the puppet show.

Melissa Buben/grade 8
Central Middle School, Columbia Heights

HOW TO REMEMBER

You walk down the path of the old north woods, just as the sun peeks over the trees. With the dew clinging to the leaves, you remember the tears that are shed when you leave. As you pass by the old rotted tree, its fragrance calls out for you to stop. Do not stop, and be warned; the old tree just reminds you of your house in town, with its yellow color, the shingle-down roof. Mama's old rocker. Papa's old cane.

Walk along in the freshness of morning with the birds singing love songs to everyone. It echoes back to you as you walk still deeper into the woods. As the smell of grass soon turns to must and the sound of the birds seems to stop, you come to that place where everything stands still.

The old fire. How well you remember it. After all, it was you who started it. As you walk through it, touching the brittle smooth blackness of the trees, you remember the vivid colors of the leaves. But now there are no leaves to be seen. All have died and fallen to the ground. No crisp crunch or snap is heard while you walk. Suddenly you stop. There's no reason to go on. The forest ends here, where the fire started. As you look at the mess, destruction and waste, it all comes back, that dreaded old memory.

The faces of nature cannot be silenced. I did it, I did it, you yell. Then run swiftly, not taking the path, to a place where life still exists. Your run through the meadow, under the trees, but then you meet up with that old rotted tree. It does no good to run or flee. They know who did it and so do you. So you sit down and wait. Wait for the time when you will blend with the trees, as a just punishment.

Lara Tebelius/grade 7
Central Middle School, Eden Prairie

OLD CHICKEN COOP

Back in the yard there's an old cricketty chicken coop
filled with spider webs.
Karen is my friend—
We got hot water and cleaned it top to bottom.
We sat in there smelling the old hay around us
and remembering the time that there were chickens in here.
We could almost taste the sweet smelling summer.

Andrea Bruchu/grade 5
Bayport Elementary School, Bayport

I have learned to go back to the house on the corner where the
people have left for the evening, to see a once only opera.
I walk the tarred streets and come to the blue-green house
with white trim. As I enter the yard, my cat, Tina, comes
to walk among my legs. I hear the soft purring. The steps
I now climb are cracked and chipping, the morning
glories closed 'til morning. The bronze doorknob turns,
and emits a tiny click. It creaks open
to reveal a room with a rocking chair against the
south wall. The red wallpaper contrasts a grandmother,
slowly rocking. The rhythmic creaking is a lullabye to
a small sleeping baby in swaddling clothes, speaking
to the old woman in dolphin-like tones, clicks, screeches,
and phrases of mourning. The grandmother is dressed in
a white nightgown and pink slippers with the frayed fur
and grayish soles. The gray-haired grandmother responds to
the baby-talk of the child. She is reading a story. The
story of the three bears, according to the cracked, discolored
cover. I step forward, and see now that the child is
me, the dull-garbed woman is my now-dead grandmother,
Nana. The child looks up at me and smiles.

Ken Gust/grade 6
Epiphany Education Center, Coon Rapids

THE SUN

The sun is a cookie
just taken out of the oven
still hot, still flaming
The sun is a pom-pom
whirling and cheering
It is the fiery eye of a cat
sly and cunning
The sun is a decorated plate
serving the hors d'oeuvres of a king
The sun is a scoop of orange
sherbet melting in the universe
The sun is the marigold of the sky

Risa Weidman/grade 6
Breckenridge Elementary School, Breckenridge

HOME

Home is three
different kinds of horses
corralled together
breaking out and going
different ways, never
getting back together
but seeing each other
in distant fields.

Bob Dailey/grade 9
Bar-None School, Anoka

This is a picture that I drew of myself, sitting in my bedroom rocking chair, next to the brown wooden doll house my dad built me. The doll house looks much bigger than it really is, and I look much older than what I drew. This room is on the top floor of a yellow house with black trim, in Rogers, Minnesota. From it I see my old bed, with the pink and white bedspread, my shelf with all the statues on it, and my white dresser. In the winter I read in it a lot, at night it is very dim. The sleeping dog is named Peanut. She spends her days playing with her rubber ball; she spends her nights sleeping on the end of my bed. There are many places where I feel like a stranger, but I always feel at home, here in the old rocking chair.

Jayme Zachman/grade 4
Rogers Elementary School, Rogers

THE BARN

In no time I have aged the
barn stark gray. The barn
stands out so much. It seems
so old it just sits there with
the wind. With no food to
eat no water to drink. Its color
shows its loneliness. It watches
the pond while it dies off.
It makes a lonely sound when it
squeaks. Mice crawl in it
and cows try to stomp on them.
The barn seems as though it
was alive. Its bones break and
cave in while it gets older. Then
its body gets well. And soon
it loses its color as it
dies and slowly slowly the
color descends. The barn's
dead heart is like a mirror.
It reflects my past, it reflects
my good times and bad times.
It shows my real self.
It reflects what I have done.

Craig Solem/grade 4
Southwest Elementary School, Grand Rapids

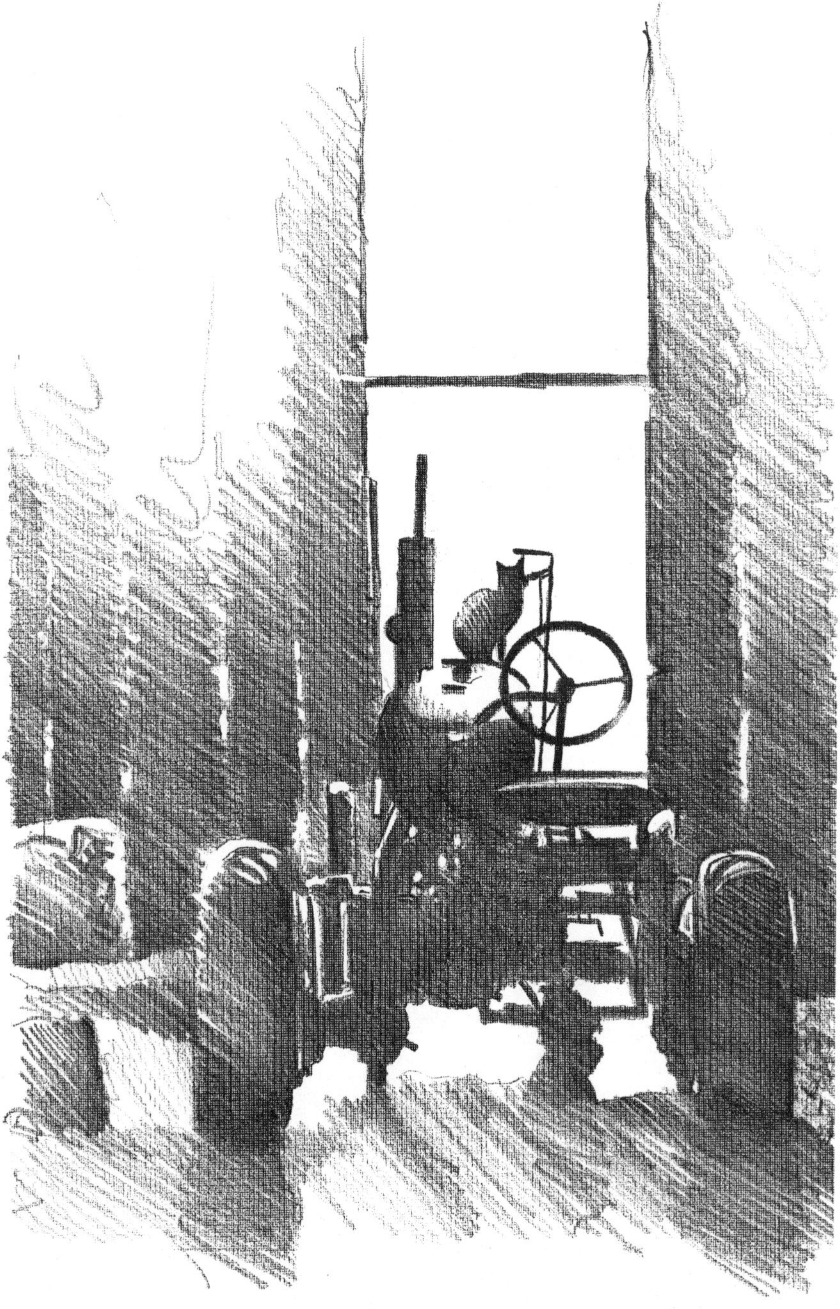

CONNECTION

Telephone wires
Spreading like
Wind in a meadow
Telephone wires
Voices carried through
Like birds flying south
Telephone wires
Connected everywhere
Like ivy on a wall
Telephone wires
Holding the world together
Like a ball of string
Telephone wires

Hello?

Jenny Woods/grade 6
Roosevelt Elementary School, South St. Paul

ON THE FARM

One sunny morning with the sun nice and yellow in the sky I ate breakfast and had scrambled eggs with grape juice and got my clothes on and went to the chicken house and shut the light off and picked up the eggs and gave them water. Then when we were done milking the cows my dad and mom would argue about if we had enough hay or not and they would talk about next month with the snow and storms and I would go and ride my red bike with a black seat and ride a long way.

Brent Kubat/grade 5
Wilson Elementary School, Owatonna

GRAND CANYON

I look down and see nothing
I look again and see
Everything.

Sheri Byrne/grade 7
St. Columba School, St. Paul

MY OLD TRUCK

My old truck sits like
a rock deep in the woods
near our home. Nobody touches
it. Nobody bothers it. It
just has a home in the woods
of its own. Animals may
creep around it as if it were
some new thing. But they
usually live as normal as
we but in their own way.
They search through woods
for food, while we go to
buy it in a store. So every
night I take corn, hay and
water to the old truck, so
when they come to look
at this amazing thing
they can eat peacefully
and without searching for
food. I like my old truck
because it has no care,
even though it seems
it does. It seems to care.
It seems. It does care for me,
for the animals who come
and see him every night

and look at him in
amazement. It seems
he is alive, way deep
down inside of him.
It does seem he has love
for the animals and me.

*Tim Kurowski/grade 5
Swanville Public School, Swanville*

ONE LONELY SATELLITE

I am the gentle giant
drifting and floating
with no ambition
no birds
to sit on me or
gentle breezes to caress
my thoughts
I lie dormant
with chains that bind
I am
the moon

*Rick Holmes/grade 11
Rosemount High School, Rosemount*

HOW TO GROW A SUN

Once I planted a blade in the spring. It took one month to grow. I fed it a cloud. You need magic words. It grew and grew. One day I woke up and I looked out the window and my sun was very big. It was up to the sky and the sky was very bright. There was no cloud in the sky.

One day the sky was dark and I could not see my sun. It was gone. I started to cry. My mother said it would come back some day. It started to rain. I cried harder. Then it stopped. I looked out of the window—my sun was out. I stopped crying. I started to laugh. I laughed and laughed. My mother laughed with me. We laughed and we laughed. The sun was laughing too. We all laughed and laughed. Then my sun started to go down. I looked at my mother and she said it's starting to get dark and the sun was smiling when it was going down.

That night I woke up and I heard something outside. I got up and looked out the window. I saw my sun. I ran to my mother and she looked outside. She said go back to sleep. In the morning when I looked out my window, I didn't see my sun. All I saw was white clean snow. I started to cry. My mother said it will come back some day. I waited and waited. It finally came back. It was happy to see me. Then my sun started to talk to my mother and father. My mom and dad could not believe it. Well, instead of doing nothing they started talking to my sun and then they started laughing. They laughed and laughed. Everybody was laughing. Then my sun was going down. It was smiling. I was smiling too. My dad was smiling. My mom was smiling too.

In the morning I saw my sun. It was prettier than ever. Then I went to school. I told my teacher that I planted a blade and it grew into a sun. She said that was good. She wanted me to write about my sun. "Sun will you come with me? I want to show you some of my friends. I want to share you. Will you go up in the sky so when I wake up I will see you and my friends will see you too?" And so he did.

Peggy Renneberg/grade 3
Rahn Elementary School, Eagan

THIS IS MY REAL LIFE

This is my real life.
Time ticks on my wrist,

a beige watch. I wear
a blue sweater. It goes well

with blue, green, gray eyes.
This is my real life,

dreaming of being a skier, and a
skater. I love Iowa, to me it's #1.

I don't really like Minnesota,
To me Minnesota is just a big city.

I will live in Iowa anytime,
it isn't just hog land, it does have cities.

My life now is boring when it used
to be fun. I love my old house in Iowa.

Parker Street was small, so was our old house,
but I will go back any time.

Tracey White/grade 5
Alice Smith School, Hopkins

THE CITY BOSTON

In Boston the morning
sky is silver gray. The
leaves are crumbling in the
wind. With cars starting to
honk. People beginning to talk.
Doors slamming, all day long.
In the evening I stop to
listen. The cars stop honking.
People's talking is stopping.
The doors close for the
last time. All that's left
are the leaves crumbling
in the wind.

Jennifer Baltes/grade 5
Glen Lakes Elementary School, Hopkins

LONDON

The shoppers hustled to and fro, hurrying in and out of shops decorated with gaudy lights and Christmas trees. The crisp air was filled with the sound of honking horns, crying children and ringing bells. As I elbowed my way through the crowd, I thought what a great place downtown London is. It had always been my fantasy to spend the holidays in Britain, and I decided to soak up and enjoy all that I possibly could. "Take advantage of this," I thought. "Pretend that you'll be dead tomorrow and observe anything and everything around you."

Moving slowly through the crowd, an old woman shifted her numerous bundles and packages to her other arm. Although the lines in her face were many and her mouth was tight, she seemed intent, occupied. She strode heavily and firmly toward the entrance to the store, and she soon became lost in the throng again.

Walking to another street corner, I saw a little boy scampering eagerly from window to window. "Look at this, Mum!" he shouted, pointing to an electric train set. He firmly pulled his mother toward the entrance, determined to convince her that he was in desperate need of a train set. I decided that I must not miss this, so I started toward the store's entrance.

The atmosphere was stuffy and crowded, yet the happiness and excitement of the season mingled pleasantly. Haughty, tight-lipped saleladies hastily wrapped packages and rang up purchases. They seemed to be made up for a Broadway musical; two spots of bright rouge, deep green eyeshadow, and eyelashes two inches long. Moving on, I noticed a line of children, all shifting their weight from one leg to the other. The cause of their impatience was obvious. Sitting on Santa's sturdy knee, the little girl told him her Christmas wishes with a happy smile and shining eyes. I remembered a time when I couldn't wait to sit on that same sturdy knee and say, "Yes, I've been good this year."

I glanced at the clock of the wall. "Darn," I thought. I was just beginning to feel at home. Supper was waiting, however, and I didn't want to delay it any longer.

The bus was just pulling out when I caught it at a run. Paying my fare, I hopped hastily into a seat. As we drove away, I remembered the last thing I had seen before boarding the bus. Endlessly moving his arm up and down, up and down, the Salvation Army man beckoned to everyone by the sound of his bell.

No one seemed to hear.

Molly J Harten/grade 10
Mankato West High School, Mankato

TRAIN CITY

The musty smell of my grandpa's train.
The hills and little houses and swimming pools.
The people like the mailman and policeman.
The 40-year-old cars and stop-and-go lights.
The train and its loud whistle.
The cold room with its soft bed and the
bubbling water distiller.
Grandpa telling me to slow the old train down.
We wish we could stay longer, but "Supper's
ready" when we just get going.

Dan Fritsche/grade 5
Lakeaires Elementary School, White Bear Lake

I AM HEALED

I am healed by:
The birds singing in the summer breeze.
The leaves growing on beautiful,
beautiful trees.
The cat's soft fur.
I am healed by:
The flowers blooming out of the
soft ground.
The dog's whiskers full of delicious maple.
I am healed by the racoons building their
winter home.
The style of the slowly moving wind blowing
through my fingers.
The jackrabbits running through my snowy
backyard.
I am healed by the food my mother
cooks for supper.
I am healed by my father going to work
with his beautiful black suit.
I am healed by half of the things in the
world.

Bobbie Jo Huss/grade 4
Thomas Edison Elementary School, Moorhead

MARY: Welcome to Herbert's Happy Hip Hamburger Haven. What'll it be?

BILL: I'll have a burger and a coke. Oh, and I also have this coupon for a free order of fries.

MARY: Uh, sorry, but did you read the fine print? In order to redeem the fries you must buy 5.8 Hamburger Surprises and 3.00152 cokes.

BILL: Oh, in that case I have another coupon that gives me a free coke.

MARY: Sorry, but you have to be eighteen or older.

BILL: But, I *am* 18.

MARY: Yes, but you have to be from out of state and have gone to Glendive, Montana at least three times, been bitten by a crab from the Pequot Lakes Annual Crab Races, and have tried, but not succeeded, in throwing a 1978 penny across the Snake River.

BILL: Well, I read the coupon and have done all those things.

MARY: That's fine. However, this coupon expired 21 days, 13 hours and 10 seconds ago.

BILL: Stick it in your ear.

Robert Goldberg/grade 6
Blake Middle School, Hopkins

THE FOREST

Crossing the small creek,
walking into the huge cottonwood forest,
hearing the soft crunch of autumn leaves,
listening to the last of the robins chirp.
The fawns look like dogs on stilts.
The knotted trees look like twisted brown rope
and they are as bare as an empty cement room.
Chipmunks are busy working on storing food,
like a grandmother canning fruit.

Andy Flint/grade 4
George Washington Elementary School, Moorhead

When you stepped into Louis Prescott's room, it was like a great mouth swallowing you up into another place and time. It was like any other room with four large walls and a single window that might remind you of a single star in the sky, among Louis' mass of cluttered junk.

In his room he had bottles of smelly, dead insects of all varieties, a box full of rusty and ancient bolts and screws, pieces of colored glass that were worn smooth, old and splintered hammers, multi-colored stones and pebbles, dirty scraps of wood, rusted and bent nails, a pile of colorful pieces of cloth, and so much other junk it was impossible to name it all.

Louis' immense (and smelly) collection covered up all of his walls and a good deal of the floor.

Louis was a stubby, six-year old youngster who kept himself occupied collecting odds and ends in alleyways and dark streets.

The room's musty and eerie smell kept his mother away from cleaning it. But no matter how much Mr. Prescott threw away, Louis' immense pile of garbage grew and grew, like a balloon blowing up.

"I love junk!" Louis sang. "There's nothing nicer than something useless."

"There's something I MUST tell you, son," Mr. Prescott told him happily. "We're moving to an apartment. You'll have to get rid of all of your 'collection' before we leave tomorrow."

"What?" Louis screamed and fainted.

While he was unconscious, Mr. & Mrs. Prescott had a rummage sale.

Keiko Sugisaka/grade 6
Armstrong Elementary School, Cottage Grove

In the sea
there was a flash!
Lightning blew up the world.
A lost ship was the survivor
of the explosion of
the world.
The ship rocked over and
sank into the
bathtub.

Nick Kuklok/ grade 3
Salem Hills Elementary, Inver Grove Heights

AN EXERCISE IN DIGRESSION

The train is waiting,
Here it pauses.
It's warm light flashing
On the houses.
Short sound of hissing
From air escaping,
And the dull rumble
That's never ending.
Tug my mind towards
My old home.
To where I listened
To freight trains moan
Back where I stayed
In the midnight,
And thought of drinking
During daylight.
My cold beer bubbling
up in glasses.
But then the memory
Fades and passes.
Leaving me listening
To the pounding.
To thick strong pistons,
And their slapping.
To crank shafts humming
From their spinning.
It leaves me looking
At lights sweeping.
The warm lights flashing

On the houses.
Now the train idles,
As it pauses.

>   *Fred Fremgen/grade 12*
>   *Bemidji High School, Bemidji*

I AM THE UNIVERSE

I sit and sit all night long.
I never grow at all.
I have always been here.
I was never born,
for friends I have none at all.
They are all inside of me.
The moon and sun and all the stars too
whom I can't see at all.
There's always night and never day
for the sun that makes day is inside of Me.
So you see I am very, very lonely.
I am everywhere. No one ever
comes, for they are in me.

>   *Nathan O'Connor/grade 3*
>   *Sunny Hollow Elementary School, New Hope*

IVORYOUS

The city of Ivoryous is made out of ivory. Upon entering
the beautiful mammoth tusk door, you notice the city
is highlighted with gold. The walls of Ivoryous are smooth
as pearls but the overall smell of the city is foul with
the fumes of decaying elephants. In the distance,
over the hills, a bull elephant screams his cry
of mourning.

Out in the open fields a lone elephant defends
against the clanging of swords of men. There is no hope.
The townspeople cry themselves to sleep among the
trumpeting. They fear their leader. He, himself
gouged by an elephant at age 15, has sought revenge
til the last beast has fallen.

The weather is bleak, no tunnel of escape for anyone.
Time here is counted by deaths, not days.

Steve Ochry/grade 9
Detroit Lakes Junior High, Detroit Lakes

ART AND THE HIDDEN DOOR

III

SELF PORTRAIT

I am a puzzle showing a peaceful mountain scene.
A man started me about fourteen years ago.
He left me, and promised he'd see me later.
Before he left, he took a piece of me with him.
I hope it was to remind him to come to me.
I sometimes wonder if he'll ever come back,
and put that final puzzle piece in.
I'm afraid that if he doesn't,
the rest of me will fall apart.
Oh why did he take that most colorful piece?

Caroline Thomson/grade 8
Central Middle School, Columbia Heights

A HIDDEN DOOR

Death is like a hidden door
waiting for someone to open it.
Just like our black lab Gypsy
waiting on the road for us to return.
Then he found the hidden door
and opened it.
Where did he go?
Why did he go?
Was it meant for him?
Death is like a rolling stone
going over the land.
Someday I will find
the hidden door and open it
and see Gypsy
waiting for me.

Julie Athman/grade 4
Rice Elementary School, Rice

I have a book inside of me.
It is open, the words are bleary
and tired, it is forever lasting,
never willing to stop.

I have a bear inside of me,
It is thriving for people, its teeth
are long and narrow, its paws
are like a pine needle, looking
for a tree to sink into.

I have a wall inside of me.
It is blocking me from outside.
It is telling me not to stray.
I try, I want, but it is unwilling
to give in.

I have a squirrel in me, I'm
always prepared, I'm full of
light, never dying in the dark, I'm
like a candle, I stay full and secure.

I have a rugged horse in me,
he is stubborn, like a
chair that cannot move,
he is greedy, but will give
if you give to him.

Connie Sutherland/grade 6
Warba Elementary School, Warba

MY LEFT HAND'S IMAGE

My right hand doesn't love life.
It doesn't work hard.
It floats like dust on
a windy day.
My left hand works so
hard,
as hard as the sun
tries to shine bright.
It wears a pretty ring
that glows in the
darkness.
It has an image to
live as long as the
soil caresses the
earth but my right
just wants to float
like dust on a windy
day, then die.

Alisa Richetti/grade 5
Gatewood Elementary School, Hopkins

WHAT IF IT WENT ON LIKE THIS FOR WEEKS?

1. What if an army man lost his way?
2. What if his radio broke?
3. What if he was losing control?
4. What if he ran out of gas?
5. What if an enemy was shooting at him?
6. What if his parachute had a hole in it?
7. What if he fixed the hole?
8. What if when he got to the door it was jammed?
9. What if he had to jump out the window?
10. What if he landed in a tree and stuck on the branch?
11. What if the branch was 20 feet off the ground?
12. What if the branch started to break?
13. What if it bent down and was nine feet off the ground?
14. What if the string on his parachute broke and he fell?
15. What if an enemy was going to drop a bomb?
16. What if he tripped on the stem of a plant?
17. What if the bomb was heading right for him?
18. What if he rolled?
19. What if the bomb landed three inches away from him?
20. What if his gun was jammed?
21. What if three weeks later the war ended?
22. What if he went home and found out his parents died a year ago in a car accident?
23. What if his girlfriend moved and he had no money to buy a house or any kind of protection?
24. What if everyone he was related to lived far away?
25. What if he met an old friend and became his roommate?

26. What if he found a job and used his friend's car?
27. What if they had a fight?
28. What if they fought about things and didn't get along?
29. What if it went on like this for weeks?

*Denise Holmes/grade 4
Newport Elementary School, Newport*

THE SANDPIPER'S SONG

My poem smells like new spring flowers
Blossoming through the snow
Like fresh cut wood with
Dew dripping from it.

My poem looks like the gentle waves
Of the ocean softly splashing the sand
Like the fat birds quietly sleeping
Through the long winter night.

If you hear the seagulls cawing,
The sandpipers chirping out their song
And the turtles softly walking
Through the sand, then you will know
It is my poem.

My poem tastes like a chocolate
Candy bar melting in your mouth
Like a tender piece of chicken with
Barbecue sauce.

My poem feels like sand sifting
Through your feet as you walk.

This is my poem.

Karen Cooper/grade 4
William Byrne Elementary School, Burnsville

A TIME OF DEATH

Lance Cranford was just getting home when the phone rang. He ran to his room to get it. "Hello?" he said, out of breath.

"Lance, this is Rod. The gang is getting together at the old grain elevator and we wanted to make sure you'd be there."

"Don't worry. I'll be there," he said and hung up. After dinner, Lance went up to his room and locked the door. He grabbed an old sweater and tore the sleeves off, then put it on. Then he took a knife and put it in his sock. After all this was done, he charcoaled his face, grabbed his gun and left.

Lance took the bus to the mall and got off. It was a long walk to the elevator, but he had the time. Ahead, he could see the bulky shape of the elevator looming in the distance and behind him he could see light coming from the mall.

Block after block he walked, but his instincts suddenly told him to run. He started running towards the elevator and safety. He could hear the sound of tires behind him. As he started running faster, he could feel the warm blood running down his ankle from the knife in his sock and the tears of fright running down his face.

He heard the sound of footsteps behind him, turned around and pulled out his gun. His follower, seeing the gun, ditched behind a dumpster nearby. Lance looked around and, seeing nothing, turned around and ran. Then, a click of a trigger cocking. A shot. Then, a cold scream of death. As he was falling, Lance caught himself on a hydrant and slowly sank down, sobbing and moaning.

People started to gather. Then a lady, seeing blood, screamed. The last sound Lance heard was the wail of sirens and the sound of laughing from behind the dumpster. Lance Crawford was dead.

* * *

I watched from behind the dumpster as they lifted the body into the ambulance. Then all I could hear was the sound of sirens in the distance and the sound of kids yelling, "Hurry up, Lance," coming from the elevator.

I took my murder weapon and tossed it in a creek nearby. I walked down an alley and could sort of sense Lance about, but I didn't care. He was dead and that's all I wanted.

I walked up Maine Avenue to the harbor and watched the fishermen unload their catch. I must have fallen asleep, because when I opened my eyes, it was bright out. The sun pierced my eyes, but I dug in my coat and found a pair of shades.

At lunch, I went home and grabbed a bottle of beer. I went to my room, locked the door and opened the window. I saw Mr. Gullenferd raking his yard and I launched bottle rockets at him. Swearing, he ran into his house and the next thing I knew he came out, pulled out a hand gun and shot me. I was hit in the head but I couldn't really tell. I felt my head and touched a glob of brain oozing out of a hole in my head. I lay down but when I did, it caused my body to twitch.

At 3:00, I died, but I appeared in a hellish nightmare. I was in what seemed to be a stone chamber with a ceiling of flame. I walked through a door and entered a room which contained a bench. I moved closer. A corpse seemed to be sitting on the bench. The door closed behind me with a slam. The corpse's eyes were fixated on me and I was frozen with fright. The corpse just sat there with a sad look on his face. Then he laughed. I looked closer and saw who it was. It was Lance. I ran towards the door and started banging. I could still hear laughter and I kept banging. Then he stopped so suddenly, I froze. I looked to my side and I was face to face with a corpse—the corpse of Lance. He looked at me and said, "Now you'll know how it feels." He pulled out a gun. Just then, a door opened but I couldn't move. He pointed the barrel at me and cocked the trigger. "You'll soon feel eternal death and pain forever." He pulled the trigger and I screamed, a cold scream, a scream that would last for all infinity.

Russell Boebert/grade 7
St. Thomas Academy, St. Paul

SUNRISE

Stroke by stroke the tip of my
brush gently brushed against
the paper. A sudden roar left the canvas
as the airplane soared softly in the air.
All that was left was an empty
space on the canvas. The beautiful sun
was rising up softly, glistening like a pretty
gem, with the horizon just floating there
like no one cared. The sky was beautiful,
filled with gleam. Why is there no
one in the picture? Who is in the airplane?
No one knows.

Brad Schwartz/grade 5
Meadowbrook Elementary School, Hopkins

SCHOOL'S OUT

I.

Run down by a mad driver
In the prime of life

We all felt her loss:

Sadly baying hounds felt it
Revealing their sadness to the stars

In the morning
Sweetly singing birds
Brought forth their eulogies

Even the winds
Had calmed themselves
To allow her passing

II.

She wasn't paying attention
When she crossed the street

We're going to miss her
For at least a month

Her dog was out the next
Night
To mate

The sparrows and the starlings
Fought
Over the tree in her front yard

It was 90 degrees in the shade
And not a hint of a breeze

Scott Dolan/grade 11
Park Senior High, Cottage Grove

MOON BOOKS

A moon book is a
book that has craters
outlined with words,
it is a circular book
that knows everything
about space, it goes
around a giant dictionary
and that goes around
a giant encyclopedia.
It is thick because
it is a very big book.
God always reads it,
it is a spelling book,
an angel of God wrote it,
bookworms slide down
the craters of it.
It tells about rocks,
sports and chemistry,
it knows about presidents.

Aaron Leichter/grade 3
Royal Oaks Elementary School, Woodbury

As we sit here the day flies by
like an airplane enroute to San Francisco.
The airplane may go back
but we can never come back to this specific day.
The clouds outside are gray and dark
like the darkness of night.
The newly fallen snow has already started
to turn to that light grayish color it gets
from the grime and pollution of the city.
How much the white snow reminds me of
my grandmother's face just before they closed the lids.
I wondered how dark and chilly it really was
down there underground.
I guess I'll find out sooner or later.
There's a chill in the air that gives you
the chills just like on a dark summer night
you are out walking around and you hear
the sounds of the crickets, then suddenly
you hear a strange sound; you stop and stare
into the darkness, you grab hold of yourself
while goose bumps run up and down your body.

Ann Bauer/grade 12
White Bear High School, White Bear Lake

ENDING

At the end of a sentence,
just one single word remains
and it's over, it's done.
Breathless, no commas,
just a period, right
at the end.
Blurry the words move together.
What does this mean?
One single sentence
stuck all by itself
at the end of the paragraph's
huge continent.
Black letters on white
grow tired of standing,
fall together and dance,
the last life on the page.

> *Su Price/grade 11*
> *Dover-Eyota High School, Eyota*

(haiku)

Somebody sneezes
and, as if they're dominoes
ev'ryone follows

> *Scot Ninnemann/grade 5*
> *Cedar Island Elementary School, Maple Grove*

I am a horse without a rider
an award everybody wants to win
a social studies book nobody enjoys

I am a song without a singer
an age nobody wants to
grow to
a kitten that is loved
a dog that is hated

I am a sun everybody hopes
to have every day
and snow everybody doesn't want
a bowl everybody licks from
a soft bed everybody jumps on

I am a poet without a poem
a deer that a hunter wants to
kill
a book everybody wants to read
a shoe that is torn and
worn down

I am a bear that is loved
a car that is washed monthly
a desk that gets slammed on
a dead fish lying on the shore
a girl without a shadow

Nina Barjesteh/grade 4
Woodbury Elementary School, Woodbury

My ears heard the untuned guitar, the untrained voice belting the songs, in the background the intense sucking of a baby on his mother's breast. My nose reacted to the odor of bodies and of unfresh breath. Standing to sing I felt the pressure of my body's weight on my feet but didn't wish to sit down on the hard wooden bench. Outside the windows I saw the movement of little children walking by and a bycycle wheel being pushed by a small boy. As I looked out I noticed the windows, they were in sections of rectangular glass with several sections missing.

The intense heat and the humidity seemed to smother me. My saliva glands worked to provide moisture. Unconsciously wiping my sweaty forehead, I heard the dark preacher begin to shout his message. As I saw the old ladies bringing out fans, I folded my Sunday School paper and began to fan myself and settle down to the typical African church service.

My thoughts drifted to more pleasant things. A Big Mac and a chocolate shake, milk and chocolate chip cookies fresh out of the oven, things from home. I wondered when we'd go back to the States, possibly soon, I thought, since the coup took place. The President and my friend's parents, both executed. Why is life so full of violence and corruption? I wanted to know. My stomach ached with these thoughts of distress.

In the distance I heard the faint sound of sirens. As they drew closer the group of fast moving cars stopped abruptly in front of the small church. Out walked some recently appointed dignitary of the new Liberian government. He, wearing his military dress uniform, and three other of his soldier aides stiffly marched into the room where we were and sat down.

Terror-filled eyes turned and stared, children whimpering was the only sound. I felt my pulse racing in every part of my body. Then, suddenly, the old preacher began to speak once more and a calm came over the crowded room. We had survived one of the many frightening crises which were to come.

Cindy Falley/grade 10
Apple Valley High School, Apple Valley

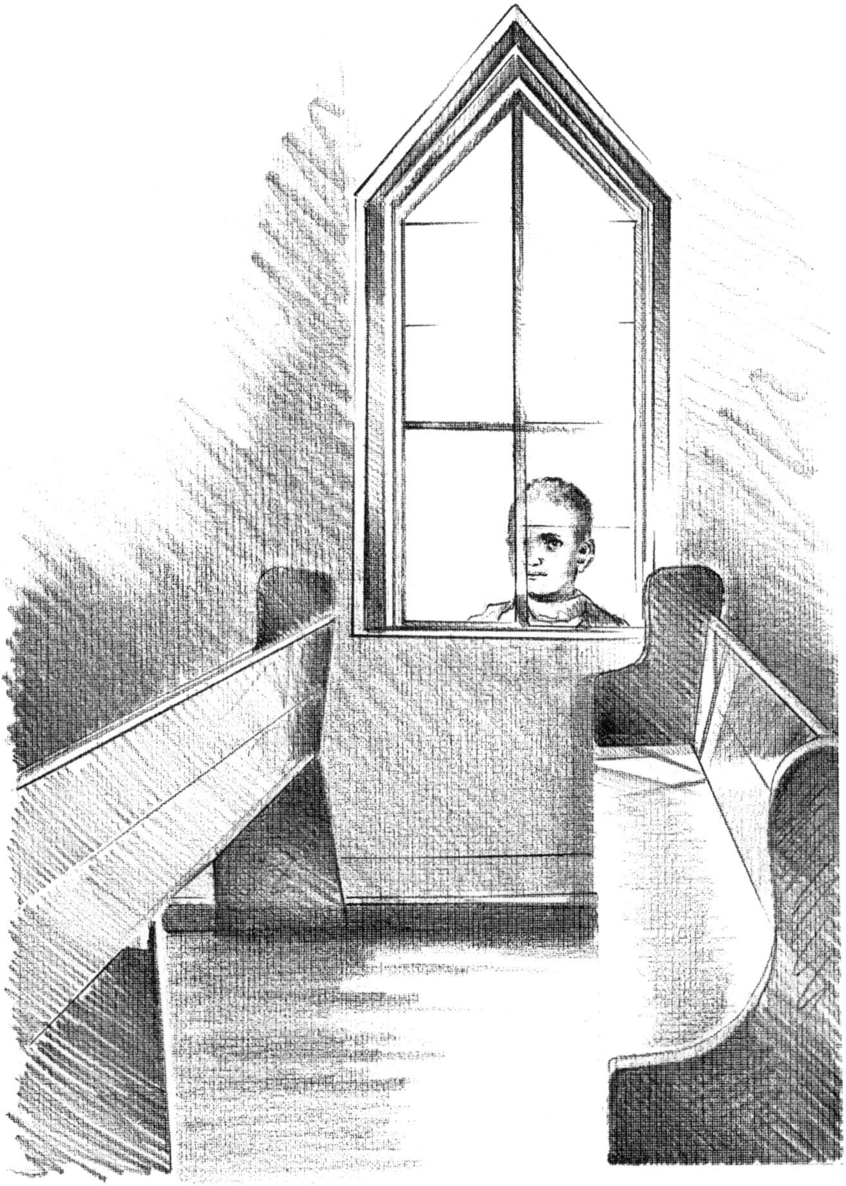

As I walk down
the street I see
the different things
surrounding me.
I'm walking in a foggy
world, everything is a dream.
The people I meet,
the faces I see, all
a blur.
I am a robot, automatically
and mechanically moving
through the halls of
life.
My memory is an old
purple sock thrown in
the attic.
I drift aimlessly
through the rooms,
bumping into the ugly
enemies.
The boob tube, putrid
green and deceivingly
red. I have been drawn
to its addiction once
too often.
My spirits soar as
an earthworm in mud.
When the day is done
and I may go to bed,
I long so much
for that magazine, or
phone call. I am an old
dusty novel waiting

to be read.
The landscape changes
color as fast as a
chameleon rolled in
crushed crayons.
My mood changes as
a goal is neared.
It was so long ago
yet so near that
I felt clear. Smells
of frying fish, the
warm, tingly sensation
of love, the taste of
success, felt so right.
Now it's nothing, it's
mixed with the other
bundles of forgotten,
smelly, discolored rags.
Will I ever see
the end of this bitter
silent road?

Maria Edington/grade 8
Franklin Middle School, Thief River Falls

The memories of the flag
that caught the bullets
of the war.

> *Bobby Foster/grade 6*
> *Colvill Elementary School, Red Wing*

Death is like a test you
didn't study for.

> *Jeff Ukestad/grade 6*
> *Hillside Elementary School, Cottage Grove*

If a tuba was made out of moonlight
its brass mouth would move all the time
bragging about its lovely music
and then the clouds would be sick!
The sun would be sick!
And the moon would be put in jail!
I'm glad that there is no tuba made out of moonlight
because I don't want the moon in jail!

Rachel Reksten/grade 3
Howe Elementary School, Minneapolis

WHEN WILL I DIE . . .

In me I am as clear to be seen as
the clearest lake I know of . . .
The clearness in me is as calm as
can be; in it there are fish and
soft pebbles of sand doing a
gentle dance for me . . .

And in me there is the roughest water-
fall I know of . . .
the roughness in the roughest water-
fall I have in my hit toward another
person, toward my enemy or even
the ape in me . . .

The ape in me is as strong as I
can be when I can't break the
bars to let me free . . .

I have a flower in me that the
wilderness gave me and won't take
that thorny rose away from
my heart . . .

That thorn in my heart from the
pain my mother has left just won't
go away . . . The wilderness and
my mother have put it here to
stay and never go away . . .

The love that has been handed
down from my father just won't
let go for as long as I live with
that love in me.
I will live forever . . .

Tana Stromseth/grade 6
Delano Middle School, Delano

The sounds of waves crashing to the shore fills the air. Cliffs rise high and proud above this sea. A swift breeze lifts the mist of the sea in the air, making it salty. Wet sand squishes around Donna's feet and toes as she walks along the shore. She passes a group of children building a shabby but well-intended sand castle. As a group of teenagers get out of their customized van and VW bus and unload their surfboards, blankets and an ice chest, one of the guys yells,

"Last one in the water drives the bug back to town."

They all dash for the water.

A little farther over there's a bearded old man trying to explain to a young child why he won't go into the water.

"But why won't you go in the water?"

"Cause I cain't swim."

"Well just come and sit in the water with me."

"It's too cold."

"Ah it isn't eith . . ." The child stops his protests when hears a girl screaming.

"Put me down! No, oh no, you wouldn't. Ahhh . . ."

There's a loud splash as two boys throw the girl into the water. She comes up gasping.

"Ohh, I'll get you two for this, just wait."

A painter not far from there rushes his work to capture the girl's expression.

Peggy Grant/grade 9
Worthington Junior High School, Worthington

This is for those who wake
up on the wrong side of
bed,
with their shoes untied and
their shirts on backwards.
For those who wake up from
a nap with the teacher's and
every eye on them.
For the teacher has just
directed a question toward
them.
For those who have oatmeal
around their mouth and
milk stains on their pants.
For those who hate sleeping
like silent beasts of burden
I fear for them who see no
brightness in life.
They will find no reason
to live.
For those people,
may they find some sense of
life. Like dry, rotting trees
when rain comes pouring down.

Karen Schillewaert/grade 11
Monticello High School, Monticello

FRUSTRATIONS

Too much pulp in my orange juice or maybe
A pen in the spiral of a notebook
Love at first sight
Photograph of a blurry mom with the dog

Too much ice in a glass of pepsi or maybe
Saying goodbye as if forever
Blue fingernails
The last breath of a newborn bird.

Tracy Siegfried/grade 12
Apple Valley High School, Apple Valley

(haiku)

if tomorrow melts
I would tell a little rhyme
to melt the angels

(haiku)

my dark blue sweater
and my favorite red coat
are getting married

Tami Volk/grade 6
Sky Oaks Elementary School, Burnsville

The ground was parched—it was hard and cracked. The smell of fresh blood lurked in the air. It was an awful stench. The young boy whimpered pitifully and rubbed his reddened eyes. There were grayish hills surrounding him. They looked like the stalagmites of a cave. I could hear vultures screeching their rage at the hills. They needed food and water, something which the hills had always given them. They no longer supplied these things. The dirt tasted almost bitter from its lack of water. There was a strange light becoming brighter along the horizon. It shone blindingly bright for a second, but then suddenly faded and went away. I looked towards the boy again. He slowly rose from his crumpled position. He watched as his dark shadow disappeared over the horizon.

Julie Haurykiewicz/grade 7
St. Bartholomew School, Wayzata

THE POEM NOBODY LIKES

You are the poem that nobody likes.
Your verbs hang limp and crippled
Across a lifeless frame.

Your nouns are broken dolls,
rejected, lying in the mud,
created by the rain of cloudy impressions.

The clock moves around its set path,
yet you do not change.

You are forever buried
under the scorn and misunderstanding
of those that read you.

Greg Johnson/grade 7
Plymouth Junior High School, Plymouth

DEATH

When death comes glass shall shatter.

Music shall stop.

Sunshine shall go and rain shall come.

Peace shall go and war will come.

Blood will be shed and if you go shopping you will have to have the number 666 on your forehead.

And the good shall fade in the clouds.

Jeremy Olson/grade 4
Jordan Elementary School, Jordan

Sawing cat _{in half} guts

I play my violin
S
  c
   r
    e
     e
      c
       h
        e
         s
          ricochet the walls
as I serenade the dust bunnies under the bed

Fingers trudge   up and   down   the cat guts

like unpaid serfs
plowing the lord's fields

    v
     i
    b
     r
    a
     t
    t
    o
     sounds like a w^ap^ed record
                 _r

being played on mono

Mary Sharratt/grade 12
Jefferson High School, Bloomington

GREEN

I
If I die
smile when you see green
    (I have smelt the newly
    cut grass after it has
    been mowed)
        My 10 speed waits in the garage
    (I can see a girl riding
it down my driveway)
    If I die
    smile when you see green
    If I die

II
    Green swims in the green city
pool. Green never asks, "how
much green?"
    Green walks through the
greenest of all greens
    Green saw me standing
in the neighbor's corn field.

III
    The green of Italy, the
green of Paris, the green
of Saskatchewan,
    the green of lettuce, the
green of leaves

IV
    Green was there during
the 49 gold rush, green was
there to touch Julius Caesar's

garland, green was
there to smell the first
thanksgiving feast.
 Green is in El Salvador
fighting with the soldiers.

V
 Green, light green, dark green,
aqua green, blue green, yellow green,
olive green, green of fern,
bright dreary green, oh
happy irrelevant green.

VI
 Green turns highways
into rivers, rivers into deserts,
green turns poverty into wealth,
paper into greenbacks.

VII
 Green is Columbus, Pocahontas,
Green is Lincoln, Romeo and Juliet

VIII
 Why does green come to frolic
with the desert sun?

IX
 Go far away, where the
green wallpaper is faded to
the lightest brown,
where the freezing temperatures
constantly blow the tundra
land over with snow, never
destined to be warm and
green.

Yet go further, when
green was farmed by
long forgotten farmers,
　　　when green was
bountiful and men were
scarce.
　　　Yet go even farther
when the last green has
outlived the rest and has
known green solitude.

　　　　　　Julie Krueger/grade 11
　　　　　　Orono High School, Long Lake

MY FAMILY
IS A BOX OF CRAYONS

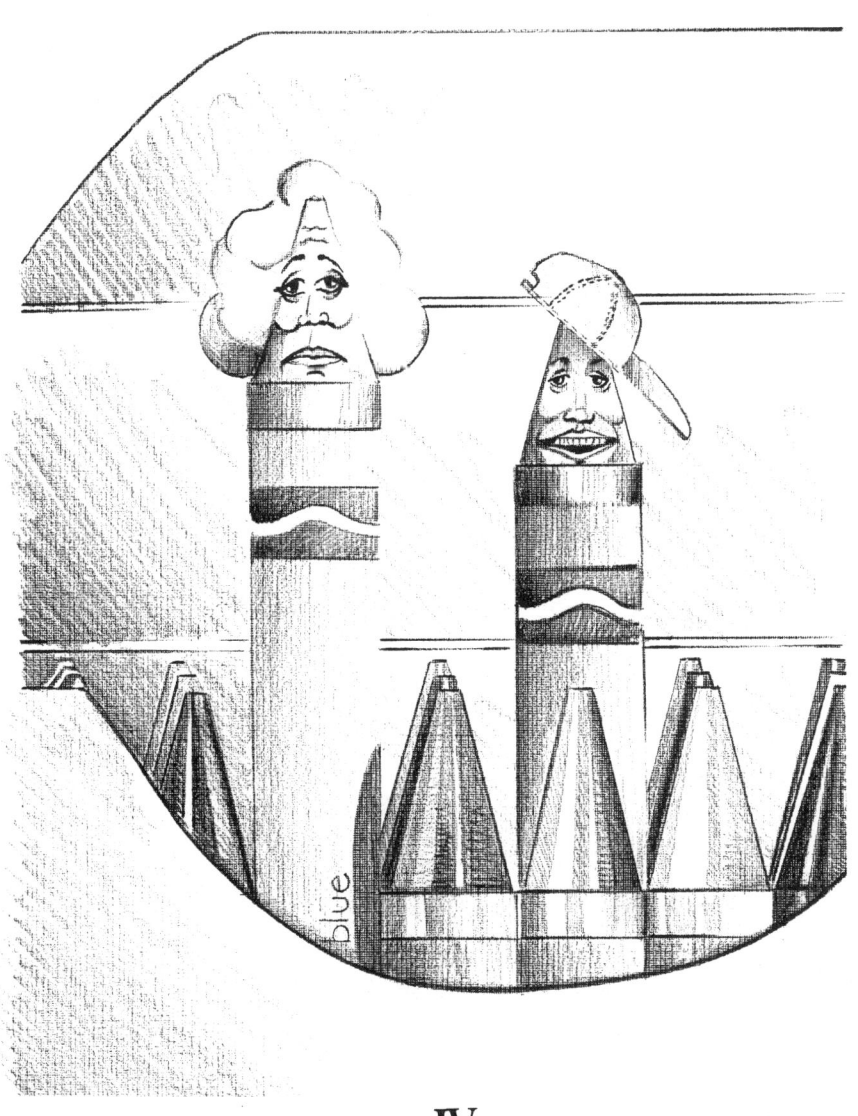

IV

MY FAMILY IS A BOX OF CRAYONS

My family is a box of crayons.

My mother is blue because she is mostly sad.

My father is red because he is mostly mad.

My sister is orange because she is mostly happy.

My brother is purple because he is mostly wild.

I'm lots of colors because I'm happy, sad and mad and wild.

Stephen Marsh/grade 1
St. Mary of the Lake School, White Bear Lake

The lemonade is getting watery,
ice cubes melting down.
There won't be much this year,
not much at all.
Still, it's ours.
50 acres a lot in this town.
No more mortgage on the house.
Bad time. Bad time all around.
But my mama farmed
and my daddy farmed and
the hot wind didn't do nothing
but make them old.
It blew wrinkles on their faces.
Don't want to be old . . .
but I guess I already am.
Sun's too hot,
call him in from the
field.
Feed him,
in a minute.
Lemonade's getting warm.
Better drink it.

Kris Hansen/grade 10
Harding High School, St. Paul

DUSTY TV

An old TV sitting
in the basement. Its
screen all dirty and
dusty. As I sit and
look at it, it reminds
me of the first time
it went out. We were
watching Scooby Doo
and then like the sun
setting it slowly went
out. It was my sister's
and I really never noticed
it sitting down here until
we cleaned. It's like
some things we don't
notice until we really
see them and miss them.
The color of the set
is black and white
but I could tell the
color of Woody Woodpecker's
body. I was only 4
years old when it was
still alive, but I
remember I would
climb up on my
sister's lap. Because I
was so small she could
put her chin on my
head. But then it was
time for me to go
to bed. The next morning

I went to turn it on
and it stopped. I knew
it had just done the
same thing my grandma
had done when she
died, the TV's battery
wore out, and my
grandma's heart stopped.

Kari Frechette/grade 6
Wyoming Elementary School, Wyoming

A DAISY

I want to speak for my brother,
my brother is special like a spring
daisy poking his blossoms out of the snow,
people that don't know him think
of him as an alien, in exile, that
doesn't belong, or deserve to
be out of doors.

My brother has a problem, a
disease that cannot be cured,
he can be taught but many
people do not know
how to teach my daisy, my retarded
brother.

Shane Johnson/grade 7
Grandview Middle School, Mound

Me and my grandmother would always make
a trek down the musty smelling road,
the trees hung with Spanish moss
reaching down like long fingers
over to a round pond, rippling
in the light breeze. We would call
loudly to the ducks rounding
the other side. They would come
over, squawking loudly for the
bread we threw. The geese, unwelcome
but unavoidable, would snatch the
bread from our fingers before
we could feed it to the shy ducks,
hiding in the background.

Helena Kriel/grade 6
Breck School, Minneapolis

WAXING

He begins to strip off last year's wax with a blow torch and a scraper. His large, white eyebrows lower with every pass of the scraper. After awhile he wipes down the trusty skis with an old, torn rag. Next, he reaches for a can of pine tar which has occupied the same spot on the dusty shelf for many years. The pine tar is applied and heated. Then he once again wipes the skis. The effort causes him to rest for a minute—catching his breath. The old, crusty wax is heated to apply new life to it, and is methodically rubbed into the shaped hickory. Two layers applied, he again wipes the skis down. Then, as so many times in the past, he puts the skis back into the closet until their next annual waxing. After checking the dusty, antique school clock on the wall, above a farmyard from the homestead days, he wheels himself back to the kitchen for a quick snack of hot chocolate and dry crackers.

His withered hands slowly transport him through the widened hall. The carpeting deadens most of the sound—except that creaking he's been meaning to fix for some time. Still that sound reminds him of his porter days in the Chicago depot pushing that large cart with all those suitcases. That job led him to so many things—advancement to ticket teller, then a manager's job in the Burlington Northern office. Then came the strike—it really wore him. He never believed in the union. Not one of those three union men will ever know how badly they hurt him. His spinal cord has been injured, paralyzing him from the waist down during a violent outbreak. If it weren't for his pension, he wouldn't survive. Hearing the local train's whistle brings back his better days; a crowded room full of people recreates the mob, he had to leave the city and move back to his home town to escape those mobs. When he returned to Northern Michigan the snow reminded him of his childhood days skiing. He wasn't the best cross-country skier around, but he was known for always having the best-prepared skis around. Now, with the new fiberglass skis on the market, his talent was fading. No longer did people he knew and even people he didn't know visit him for advice on waxing.

He awoke after a short nap to find the dishes from his snack still uncleaned—he'd do it tomorrow when it was really worth doing. He wheeled into the bathroom to check on that drip, he swore that it was the dripping of rain off the awning above the employee's entrance to the depot. His mind drifted aimlessly. When he again awoke the room was dark—the cold northwest wind was attacking the house with gust after gust.

He headed up the ramp to the floor a half-story up. It was not easy, but he could still make it up to the bedroom to get out the new wool shirt he had ordered by mail. It was so much like that shirt he used to wear to chop wood in his younger days, until coal came in. Now he never worries about fuel—oil is very dependable still, he's never used more heat than necessary.

Steve Worner/grade 11
Fergus Falls Senior High, Fergus Falls

OLDER BROTHER

You are the fog that hangs over me
    and then you drift away

I am the dew
    always left behind

        Julie Vennewitz/grade 8
        Central Middle School, Columbia Heights

MY FATHER

His silvery-gray hair is like the
feathers on the wings of Pegasus.

His big brown eyes remind me of
chocolate ice cream with that certain
way of melting.

That big broad bony frame of his
is like an ancient building that
is slowly crumbling.

He sits at that desk of his
looking almost forbidding, but still
he has a twinkle in his eye.

He can crack a crooked smile
and raise an eyebrow that can
make anyone laugh.

He plays with the kitten acting
almost like a kid.

Coming alive in the kitchen he
could be a chef.

Only if a wish could do
things, I wish he'd have a longer
time to live.

Susan Adams/grade 6
Crestview Elementary School, Cottage Grove

UNCLE JOEL

My uncle has hands as big
   as a beach ball. It sounds
   like thunder when he walks
   down the stairs.
He sits on the soft dark brown
   sofa reading magazines
   for snowmobiles or motorcycles.
   He bends over to pick up
   more magazines with
   swift strong arms.
I remember looking for agates.
   along the country road.
I want to give him the
   biggest, most beautiful
   agate that will bring
   happiness when he is sad.

John Cooper/grade 6
Caledonia Elementary School, Caledonia

MOVING

The sun shines bright
on a field full of corn.
My grandfather, with old faded
coveralls, goes out to do chores.
He turns the pump on for water.
After chores, he turns the water off.
Then he walks by fields
full of corn into the house.
Him and grandma talk.
They decide to move.
The sun shines bright
on the field while they put
their things into the truck.
They move into their new house.
He has a friend turn on
the pump for the animals.
He has a friend cut his corn.
He goes out to the farm in his faded
coveralls to sell his animals.
Then, for the last time,
he turns on the pump.
Then, with his faded
coveralls, he walks by
the field that is empty now
and the sun does not shine
anymore.

Kerry Ann Dammen/grade 5
Goodview Elementary School, Winona

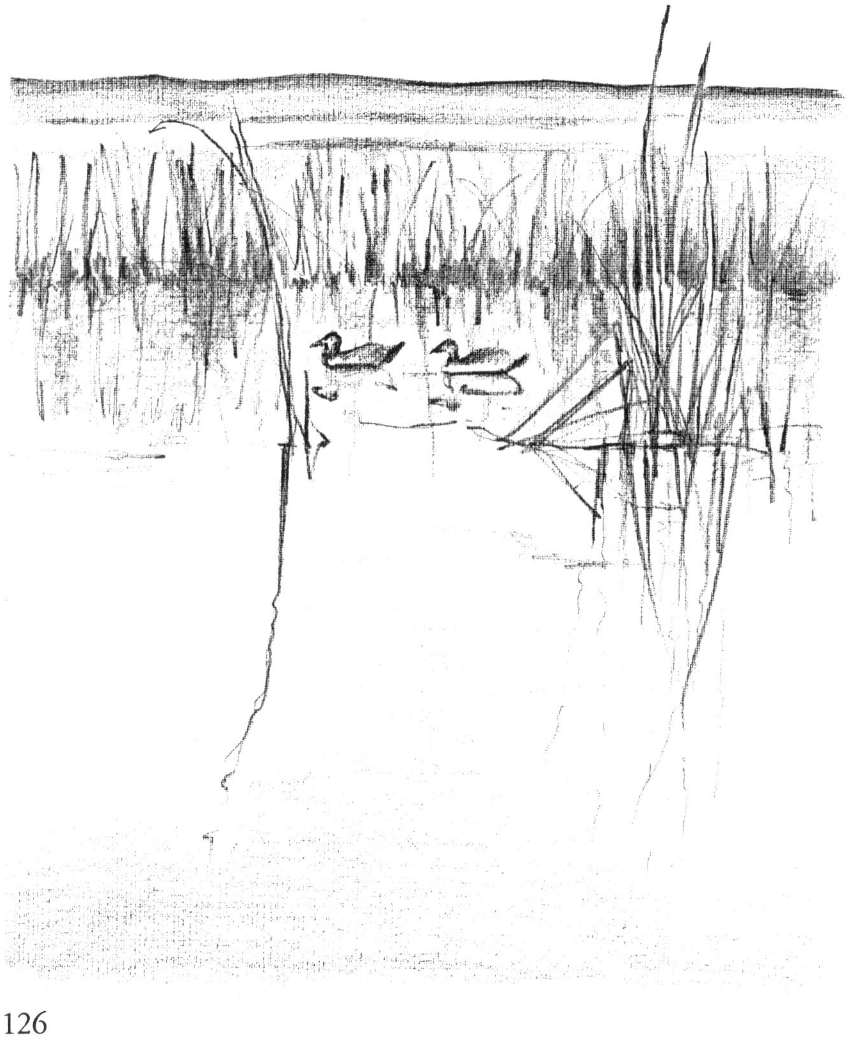

HIP BOOTS

There they hang in the garage
on a nail. I don't remember them
looking like that. I remember
the first time I used them
out hunting with my Dad.
I put them on; they were
too big and I looked funny.
We laughed and laughed.

I was out pulling in the decoys
in almost 4 feet of water.
Dad just looked at me and laughed
and, you better watch out
they might fill full of water
if you're not careful. I did not
listen, and they did. The water
made me dizzy and I fell
back. Dad saved me. Then we laughed.

Now they are hanging here
in the garage. Since then
Dad got real sick and that's
why I stopped by. I decided
why not ask Dad to go
hunting again. I told Mom
my idea. She said he has
been waiting for you to ask
all these years. I asked him,
and we went. I wore my

old hip boots and we had fun,
talked and laughed and laughed.

I had to go back to the
big city and leave him but
I said we will go hunting
again—soon. He said, I'm
always ready. The next time
I saw him was for his funeral.
I felt bad that I could not
get around to taking him
again. Mom said he waited
but you never showed up. He knew
you were busy. All he talked about
was when you took him hunting.
We cried and cried and cried.

Al Hegquist/grade 10
Columbia Heights High School, Columbia Heights

SOMEONE'S WATCHING

The air was filled with a thick mist that lingered every time it rained. The warehouse district of downtown San Francisco was dark and gloomy. The only sounds in the quiet air were of the bums and winos in the alleys and of the surf in the bay hitting lightly against the rocks on the shore. Between every street there was a row of dark alleys in between the huge warehouses which contained everything from antique furniture to the fish caught in the bay. Every warehouse district has its share of break-ins but strangely, the warehouses in San Francisco weren't equipped with any burglar alarm systems nor any night watchmen. With a war going on, none of the young men could be spared to babysit warehouses. Looking up from the alleys and backways boarded and broken windows can be seen, apparently victims of bricks, boards, or rocks.

Every night a sleezy but shrewd looking woman can be seen in the alley intersecting Third Street. She is known only as Lola. Her origin is unknown. Night after night she treks to the same warehouse. After she enters, nothing is known of what goes on inside, except by Lola and her underworld associates. She walks up the chipped cement staircase and confronts the door. She brings her soft lips up to the cool metal, and after waiting momentarily the latch on the reverse side clicks. A thick metal bar can be heard sliding smoothly against the cold door. The routine she has followed time after time is the same though this time it somehow seems different. The door opens so little that just a single beam of light escapes and falls on Lola's gazing eye. The door opens farther revealing Lola. The round head, the red lips, the smooth figure. It was Lola, the woman that looked so helpless but was a woman of power. The only other person who knew about this odd routine of Lola's was watching her tonight from the tenth floor of an office building overlooking the alley.

A knock came at the door of Hue Hogarth's office. "Come in!" shouted Hue from the inner office. The door swung open wide. In stepped a shaking woman. She was young and quite beautiful although at the moment she was looking quite unraveled. Hue looked at her in amazement. Her clothes weren't as promiscuous, but other than that she looked the same as ...... His train of thought was broken by the hysterical screams coming from the woman. "They're gonna catch me! They're gonna catch me!"

Hue immediately dropped the flask of brandy he had been drinking from and put out his cigar. He walked over to the young woman and brought her into his office. He sat her down in one of the chrome and leather chairs. He then took a seat on a pile of papers sitting on his desk. By this time the woman was practically in hysterics! "Who's going to catch you?" Hue said, trying to calm the woman down.

"The man in yesterday's paper!" She was screaming at Hue. Hue rummaged through the pile of papers he was sitting on and pulled out a copy of the San Francisco Chronicle dated October 16, 1944.

"Here's a copy," Hue said paging through to find the picture in question. "You mean this picture?" Hue asked showing the picture to the woman who had calmed down considerably from the time she had come in.

"Yes, that's him! The man that was in my room, that's him!"

"The man," Hue began, "is Max Dilton, alias Max the Mangler." That name brought back painful memories for Hue. His father was killed by Max the day before he was to testify against him. Hue, holding back his feelings, resumed reading the article. "He escaped from prison two days ago. It says he was serving an eighty year sentence for constructing a bomb and blowing up the house of a man who knew where his hideout was." Hue went on to finish the story. After returning the paper to the pile of papers he had extracted it from, he asked the woman her name. The woman sat quiet for over a minute. Hue

130

comforted her, "You needn't tell me your name, just your story."

The woman took out a package from under her coat and placed it on the desk. "This is the cause of all my trouble! Take it, please!!" Hue took the package and put it in one of his desk drawers, then sat back in his chair to listen to the woman. She began, "I was coming home from my office on Third Street. We had had an office party and I had had too much to drink, so I decided to walk to my home. It was only about 15 blocks. I was walking through the alley when I heard a crash coming from one of the warehouses. A few blocks ahead of me I found this box lying on top of a heap of glass underneath a broken window. I tried the door but it was locked so I decided to take the box home and return it on my way to work the next morning, since I would have to walk to work because I had left my car at the office. When I woke up the next morning I found a strange man in my bedroom. That man in the paper! I soon realized that he was after the box."

"So why didn't you just give it to him?" Hue interrupted.

"Well," the woman continued, "I thought that if he had followed me home to get the box and broken in to get it, that it must have contained something illegal, so I threw it out the window and I jumped out after it. Both me and the box fell into the swimming pool. I fished the box out and ran as fast as I could to your office. I had often seen your ad in the newspaper. So here I am." The woman took a deep breath and sat back in her chair.

"Why don't you stay here for awhile? You could rest on the couch while I work on finding Max," Hue suggested.

"Oh no! He'd find me here. I'll go to a place I know where he'll never find me." Hue would have offered to drive her, but he knew she'd just say no.

"Well you just go there and I'll see about getting the Mangler back in prison." With that the woman got up and slowly walked out the door.

The night had fallen on San Francisco and once again the mysterious Lola walked up to the warehouse that she went into every night. The door was open tonight so she just walked in. It was pitch black inside the cold warehouse. Lola walked over to the light switch and turned it on. In the center of the floor was the lifeless body of Max the Mangler. Surrounding him was a pool of bright red blood and a knife protruded from his chest. Lola walked up to him. It was then that she noticed the box with a note attached that read:

> Try jumping into this pool and fishing out the box, but this time you won't have to run because you won't have time! Too bad your story wasn't true because wet explosives don't explode. BYE!

As soon as she finished reading the note, the box burst engulfing the warehouse in a huge explosion. This spectacle was seen by only one person, Hue. He was in the lobby of his office building looking at his watch, it read exactly twelve midnight. Hue had some work that was unfinished. He stepped aboard the waiting elevator and reached for the control panel. Reaching up, he pushed the button marked TEN!

Tim Lander/grade 8
Valley View Junior High School, Edina

DAD

Read me, Dad.
I'm the book, you're the reader.
Don't shut me,
See what I have to say.
I'm so dusty.
Open me.

Michele Narlock/grade 4
Probstfield Elementary School, Moorhead

In diapers
barefoot and messy hair,
dishtowel in one hand,
fragile plate in the other,
there I stand on a faded
vinyl chair.
I peer into this picture
and smell the soap suds
and lingering smells of lunch.
My grandmother's house
is full of dishes and
she still embroiders flour sack
dishtowels like the one in the picture
from so long ago.
The dish from the picture is faded,
cracked and chipped now from wear
much like my grandmother.
The dish has seen home-made
hash browns, scrambled eggs, crisp
bacon, brown toast which my grandmother
still prepares when we come home.
Grandmother, I love you. Let me
dry the dishes again.

Christine Strander/grade 11
Jefferson High School, Bloomington

I am the stage, being stood and walked upon.
He is here, Bobby Boots, getting ready for his show.
He tells the jokes. I am the jokes. No!
It is me up there, I am the comedian.
Oh, really funny, thanks.
No one is out there watching.
Oh, the streets and paths I've crossed on my way up here.
Everyone laughed at my jokes, laughed at me, laughed
at my background and ambitions.
I figured well, I guess I'm ready for Vegas.
I'm up here now—the orchestra has left me without the music
Life so many times promised me.
The squinty-eyed older group of ladies
whose essence and perfume stalked me all along my way
are not out there watching either.
Where's the sweet smell? Oh. It's a joke, I forgot.
Where's the President? He should be
at this command performance.
OK Gang, show's on, ready?
What do you call a kid who's had a stinking life
but always wanted to be a great comedian, reach
every heart and eye and make them laugh, really
make them happy, just for that moment?
You call that kid a dreamer.
Wasn't that funny? Wait—who turned out the lights?

Becky Leder/grade 12
Long Prairie Public Schools, Long Prairie

THE SUN

The sun seemed to be absorbed into the gray of the ship's deck. Sparky, the big, fat, bald-headed guy, was lying on a hammock and opening a little plastic container of coconut lotion. I wouldn't dare touch those guns. They had three day's worth of tropical heat in them. I was already dark-skinned so I had my hammock in a shady part of the deck. Little native fishing boats hummed. A little distance beyond the pier, I could see the coconut palms bending to the breeze.

Ol' Captain Doob wouldn't let any of us go on shore to meet the native girls waiting for us. The native girls were selling some type of Malaysian food wrapped in banana leaves. Sure, we were able to smuggle a couple of electric fans on board during the wee hours of the night; but never any girls.

Cap'n Doob said it was against regulations of Malaysian Code 559 to allow regular combatant mariners on shore; unless they were under command of a native man, or parked off the shore of Spindle Naval Base at Wan Dung. This was due to commotion caused by the mariners when they went on shore. It seems that some drunk mariners forcibly put the ex-mayor's wife's dog to sleep.

"Hi ho!" yelled Scorpy.

"Hi ho!" I yelled back.

I liked Scorpy for his funny little abilities to weasel out of things. He was the one who smuggled the electric fans on board with a tad of help from Mishka, a native dandelion flower vendor. Mishka let Scorpy buy a couple of bushels of dandelions to scuffle the fans on deck. Cap'n Doob had one heck of a time understanding why he had to have flowers in his bathroom, on his desk, and right next to his telephone. When we were at mess, we ate in the midst of fresh flowers, planted in little coffee cups filled with water. The cook wasn't too smart, and used sea water instead of just plain water for the flowers. No wonder they turned funny colors within three hours of their placement in the cups.

Well, anyway, we all wanted to go swimming. Sure, that water looked nice; but we were sick of seeing the native kids frolicking on the beaches and having loads of fun. Swimming would be as far off the ship as we would get, and we were utterly determined to sneak out in the middle of the night and swim to our hearts' delight.

Stuart Meyer/grade 12
East Senior High School, Duluth

CREAM SEPARATOR

Out in my backyard is a cream separator.
It was given to us by my grandparents.
Whenever I look at it, I remember them.
The way my grandma makes chicken noodle soup
and fresh strawberry jam.
I think of my grandpa sitting, watching TV
turned up loud enough to hear.
I think of lying on their bed
reading old dusty comic books
with no covers.
When I look at that cream separator,
now covered with flowers, my mind
seems more at ease.

Peter Jacobs/grade 8
Woodbury Junior High School, Woodbury

   Fists swinging
punches landing
father yelling
two boys sent
to their quiet
rooms.
   I look out the
window and notice
a bird in a nearby
tree and I start
to dream that I
am a bird soaring
through the air
suddenly I hear
someone yell "you
can come out
of your room
now" but I
didn't lose the
feeling of soaring
through the air.

Brad Benike/grade 6
Sunset Terrace Elementary School, Rochester

CHILDHOOD

When I was younger I was a frog,
always going, going, going.

Now I'm a big bass
lying at the bottom of the lake.

My dad is in the boat, offering me
all kinds of different baits.

I take the bait that says
"Adulthood,"

But when I'm caught
I'm still a child.

Robbie Reed/grade 5
McGregor Elementary School, McGregor

THE SIDEKICK

I am the Sidekick,
Tonto to the Lone Ranger,
Boy to Tarzan,
never the Main Man,
the Scene Stealer.
I'm just as important
as the other guy
but I never get the spotlight.
I'm the Bartender in the Westerns
who always leaves before the gunfight—
because no one believes in me.

Troy Renslow/grade 8
John Glenn Middle School, Maplewood

THE PICNIC OF DREAMS

V

INVITE A LION TO DINNER

What I would do
if I invited a lion to dinner?
I'd sit and ask him about his
life as a child and the things
he ate. He would say dandelions and
roses, sand and seashells. I would
say, where do you sleep? In the
endless night, where the soft
sound of the owl would sing
and the soft summer
breeze would cool you. What
would I do if I invited a lion
to dinner? I would go to the
park and set out the tea and
dandelions and call it the picnic
of dreams where life is like a
baby sleeping in the weeds.

Amy Lee/grade 6
Pinewood Elementary School, Rochester

THE LONELY TIMES

You can't believe *loneliness* can enter
your own life—
It's like being in the heart of a mountain
without a single soul.
Your voice travels through mountain peaks
without any answer.
There is no movement, your mind imagines
a crow flying towards you searching for
a friend.
Your feet ache with every step in search
for someone, all that lies ahead are
roads and mountains covered with dust.
Your mouth is dry from the lack of water,
you're trying, trying, not to think of
these things.
Your mind becomes electrical, anything
could happen now, your mind is a magician.

Sharon Bachman/grade 5
Sunny Hollow Elementary School, New Hope

GETTING FAT

One night I dreamed
that I was in dinosaur ages,
but I didn't know it.
I walked down a long hill.
When I got to the bottom, I said,
"It can't be true!"
There was a steak
twelve buses long.
I started to eat it.
It tasted and smelled like
Brontosaurus, but
who wanted to know?
It tasted good
and I was hungry.
That's all that mattered.
I ate the whole thing!
I was bigger than anything.
I was so fat and big
that I could sit on a bus
and flatten it as thin
as a pancake.
When I woke up,
I wasn't hungry for six weeks.
I couldn't run
faster than the slowest turtle.
For six weeks,
it was strictly grapefruit.

Mark Swenson/grade 3
Washington Elementary School, Rochester

I am a star that hit a window at St. James School.
I am a carrot that has been eaten by
a star. And a sun that's been eaten
by mars.
I am a rocket that flies at night
and burns the hair off a dog.
You are like the moon that went
out on a date with a star.
You are a pig that eats cheese from
the moon that is gold.
You are a cow that climbed up
to the moon and married a star.
You are a horse that ate
the cheese from the moon that
is now naked.
You are a razor blade that
cut all the animals' fur off
that are now bald.
You are now a sentence that
has to leave.

Craig Uhl/grade 6
St. James School, St. Paul

MY IMAGINATION

If whales could fly upside down
then you would know what causes
thunder showers to stink

And if eyes could turn into rainbows
then noses would be lightning
with two big raindrops in the middle

And if sugar got into a fight with salt
then it would be hazardous to pies and cakes.

Jenny Belisle/grade 3
Tilden Elementary School, Hastings

The salty sea air blended in with the earthy smell of the sand. You could hear the crashing of the waves upon the shore, the screeching of the seagulls and the scream of a child. I stood there dumbfounded as the chubby little boy frantically ran from the whirlwind of sand that was floating through the air sucking up everything in its way. Suddenly it changed course and came after *me*!

The waves bounced upon the large jagged rocks. The seagulls *dived* down from the golden sky catching minnows in their sharp beaks. A thin, always moving line separated the blue of the water from the white of the sand. I ran as fast as I could; the sweat dripped from my face and evaporated, leaving my face streaked.

Later, the darkness crept up on me but I couldn't shake the whirlwind of sand. There was a couple having a campfire further down the beach under the moonlight.

The air was now cold against me because the wind had picked up, but the sand still felt warm from the bright sunlight a couple hours before.

I could hear the couple talking; the girl suddenly let out a scream—they started running in opposite directions—it still chased me.

You could hear the slapping of the waves against the rocks, the water smelled as cool as the country air after a fall rain, but the sand kept filling my nostrils and then around and around I went. I kept going around for hours then suddenly I fell onto hard ground in the middle of a forest somewhere. I walked through the forest for a couple days. Now I'm really lost.

Jodi Schmieg/grade 10
Howard Lake-Waverly High School, Howard Lake

THE WOODSMAN

A tree is falling,
a woodsman he is at heart.
He slushes through the snow
bringing the mail. He has many dreams.

Cutting wood in his spare
time
At home with a saw and
wood splitter.
Droplets of sweat run down
his face,
stream down his back.

A small brown dog bites his heel
he kicks him away,
Another receives the sweet perfume
of mace.

And he has adventurous dreams.

He used to dress as St. Nick,
I knew it was him, Santa
doesn't have a red beard.

Never put his arm around
my small frame, in praise
or adoration
Never said I love you
but I knew he did

We have enough wood for three years

This man is a stranger,
Near to my life, but still
I wonder, Does he know me?

Denise Berg/grade 11
Willmar Senior High School, Willmar

NO. II

Everyday I see a picture. The picture is a field,
a football field. It seems happy, but I feel strange
and sad. I don't know why but it just is. The sun
is shining on the field. I'm wearing a football
helmet and shoulder pads and a shirt with the Number
"II" on it. I feel strange. I hear the roar of the
crowd and the cheering. As I walk on this field, it
seems old. I am very sad, I don't know why. As I
worked my way here, I felt happy. I worked hard
enough, but this strange feeling keeps on coming.

Paul Christensen/grade 5
Montrose Elementary School, Montrose

WAITING FOR SPRING

Listen for the world to change
from darkness to light.
Dreaming of the cold snow
changing to slush.
Dressing with the feeling of warmth
on your body.
Smell the fresh wind blowing
in your hair.
Keep the feeling of the change of winter.

Matt Shuey/grade 5
Forest Lake Elementary, Grand Rapids

Let me never become a ROCK
Getting run over by cars and trucks
Being lonely
And hoping for somebody
To find me
And then
When they do
They throw me into a pond
Hoping I'll skip
But I fall down to the bottom
to drown.

Steve Schwanz/grade 6
Garden City Elementary School, Brooklyn Center

The ground is hard and cracked. I walk along in the hot climate to an oasis. I haven't had any water all day so my throat is like a sand dune. I leap toward it and all I get for my throat is a mouthful of sand! I come up to an old abandoned house and hear the wind whistling through the windows. I walk on the beach and suddenly feel a sharp pain in my foot. It feels like lightning has struck me. I find out that I've stepped on a jagged rock. My foot is cut open and bleeding like a gusher. The sand doesn't help it at all. It gets caught in my foot and stings like crazy. I sit down to rest and someone kicks sand in my mouth. It seems that all I've had to drink and eat today is sand. I lie down to rest and see paper on the sand blowing across the beach like little people marching back and forth across the battlefield. The paper blows across me and so does the sand. It gets caught in my eyes as if attracted to them. I fall asleep. When I wake up, my brown eyes are red, my blond hair is full of sand and my clothing is torn and ripped. I hate Mondays!

Cameron Black/grade 6
Fergus Falls Middle School, Fergus Falls

THE LIFE OF A DREAM

    Take a word like dream
give it a cloud in your head
    a blue sky to hang in
give it a piece of you
    and an image to create
give it happiness
    and sadness
give it time
    and a limit
give it a shadow
    for you can't remember
the happiness of a
    dream.

Carrie Beth Saba/grade 6
Katherine Curran Elementary School, Hopkins

THE FLAME

I see a flame, a flame—
blue, yellow and fuzzy.
This flame is like a peach
growing over Atlantic waters.
This flame brings me back
when fire was just discovered.
He is like me
in many ways.
He takes me places,
places I've seen before.
A war with people dying
is not beautiful.
One person I meet
lights up my life
like the flame.
The flame was always
good to me.
He always listened to me
when I had problems
and when my cat died—
He listened.
And when my mom died,
He listened to that too.
My mom, she was always
good to him.
She always lit him at night
and blew him out
at the morning sun.
I always liked the flame
until he went out.
I'm always sad
when I think of the flame.
I miss him.
I don't have anyone
to talk to anymore.

*Jason Walton/grade 7
Chaska Middle School, Chaska*

A STRANGE SWEATER

Kathy sat in her last hour algebra class. Her eyes roved the room, but they stubbornly refused to land on the chalkboard and what was written there. She heard a noise which sounded like a hundred bees searching for honey. It was only the teacher lecturing on the same material as the day before. Her eyes chose the green, flowered sweater which sat before her as their resting place. Slowly, in the pattern of the sweater, all she could see was a green, grassy hill with beautiful flowers of all shapes and colors. Their fragrance was so sweet and strong, she wanted to lie among them and think only of their beautiful sweetness. Overhead, a flock of birds was silhouetted by the clear blue sky. Kathy heard the sound of bees again. They must be gathering honey. But as Kathy looked around, she couldn't spot a single bee. Suddenly, the droning sound ceased. In its place Kathy heard a harsh voice calling her name. In an instant, Kathy's beautiful, flowered paradise was replaced by the disapproving stare of her algebra teacher. The colors before her were merely those of a gaudy sweater which Kathy herself wouldn't have considered buying.

Val Leske/grade 12
Buffalo Lake School, Buffalo Lake

         A
      kite is
    like a bird
with no head. A kite
    soars through
    the sky like
      a slave
        who

gained

his

freedom

Josh Squires/grade 4
Central Elementary, Winona

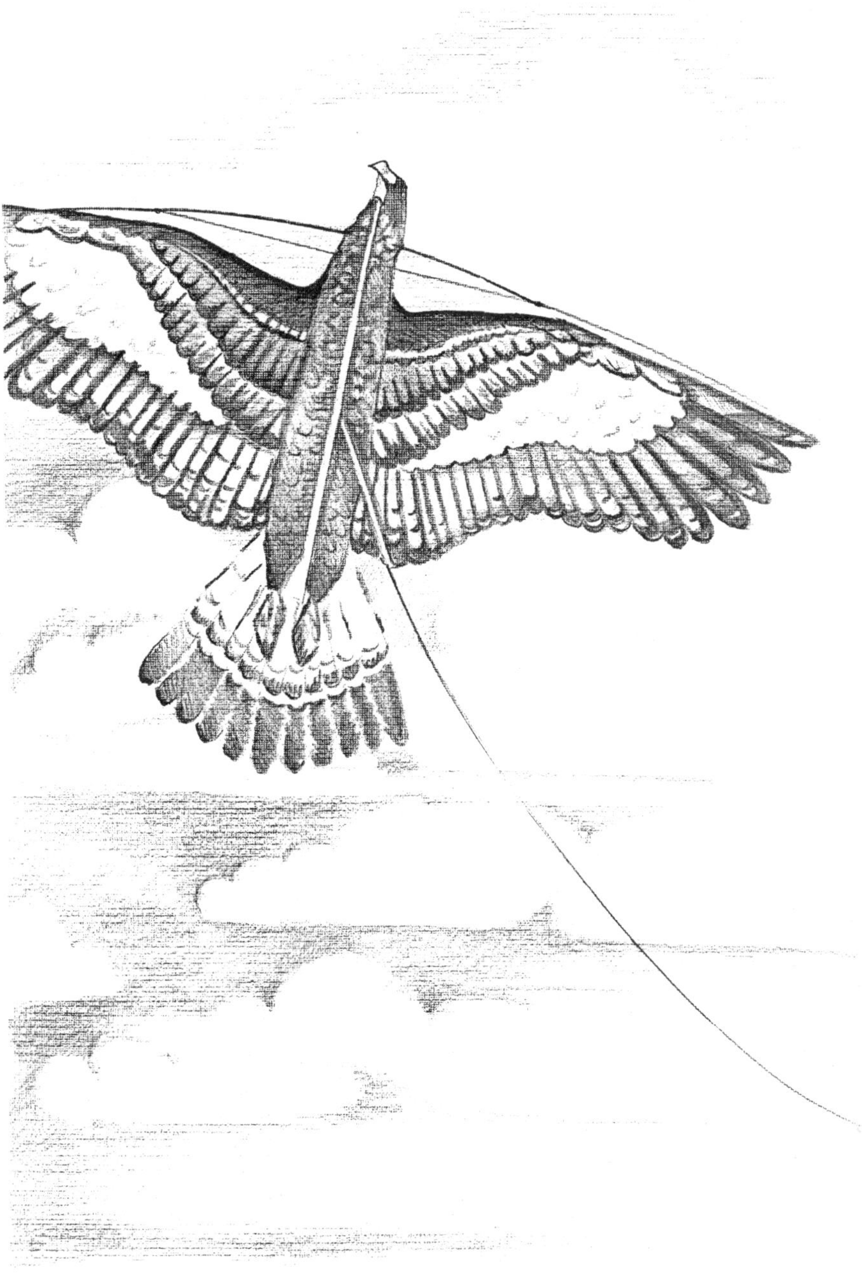

COLD WINDS AND DARK NIGHTS

Come soon, bitter stiff
winds. Blow your beautiful
white snow and may the
dark, star-struck nights
be forever.

Andrew Bonnette/grade 11
Woodbury Senior High School, Woodbury

down
go
they
times
some
lights
have
and
up
and
up
up
go
flying saucers

Joseph Hsieh/grade 1
Wilshire Park Elementary School, Wilshire Park

In my dream I dreamed that
at my birthday party someone
gave me a present. It was about
1 foot tall and about 6 inches
wide. It was wrapped in polka-dot
paper. I opened it up and there
was another wrapper. This
time it was striped and
eleven inches tall 5 inches wide.
I opened it, another wrapper.
I can't remember what it
looked like, but it was strange,
and an inch smaller each way.
Then another package and
it decreased by an inch,
then another, then more,
and more (oh, by the way
this took place in our dining room).
They kept shrinking by an
inch each way.
    Then I woke up.

Jennie Sullivan/grade 6
Cornelia Edina Alternative Program, Edina

I AM A CLOUD

I like being a cloud, I can see
the world.
I travel high on a gold escalator
and low by the silver skyline.
I may rain or snow.
I like being myself, being what I am.

Sometimes I don't like being a cloud,
because the wind blows me around.
But the angels rest on me
to guard the earth.

People imagine I am many different
things. They imagine me as
giraffes and pineapples.

I eat the rainbow after a storm,
and I nibble evaporated dreams.

Marcy Olson/grade 6
Gibbon Public School, Gibbon

TOMORROW'S DOOR

A thousand yesterdays ago
I began a journey
Crawling through carpet jungles and household mazes
Walking past red oak trees and football fields
The world sped by as I ran through time
Up hills of homework
Through valleys for holding hands
Beyond home and school and friends
Ahead there is a door
Today I turn the handle
Tomorrow I walk through
Alone

Tom Gibbons/grade 12
Grand Rapids Senior High School, Grand Rapids

MY DREAM

Once I dreamed that I was walking
on the flag.
I came to the stars.
When I walked on a star,
I went to that place.
The first star I stood on
was Minnesota.
Before I knew it,
I was standing by the State Capitol.
Next, I went walking on the calendar.
When I stood on number one,
I was one year old
and when I stood on number eight,
I was eight again.

Liz Bamberg/ grade 3
Cleveland Elementary School, Fergus Falls

LAURA

It was a hot day in July and my family and I were at our cabin in northern Minnesota. I decided to go on a walk in the woods where it would be much cooler. I started down the dusty road. I stopped suddenly to watch a young doe nibbling silently on some juicy, red berries.

Drip! Drip! Drip! It was starting to rain and here I was in the middle of the woods. I knew I wouldn't be able to get back to our cabin without getting thoroughly drenched. I ran farther into the woods and found a strange cave. It had wet, muddy walls, a dirt floor and a stinking odor. Oh well, at least I was dry. I wandered through the cave and found a little girl asleep on the floor. She awoke and looked at me curiously. I quickly introduced myself and asked if she was staying somewhere around here with her family for the summer. "Oh no," she said. "I don't have a family." "Then where do you live?" I asked. "And what's your name?" "My name is Laura and I live here," she answered. "Here?" I exclaimed. "In this old cave?" "Yes," Laura answered. "Come on, I'll show you around."

As Laura talked to me I noticed her green eyes. I'd seen green eyes before but not like hers. They were so bright. Laura led me into the next room. It was so different from the other room! It was beautiful! It had marble walls, a smooth, wooden floor and a smell like roses. There were paintings on the walls and flowers everywhere. "Wow!" I said, "This is great!" Suddenly I heard a crashing noise. I ran out of the cave and looked around. A tree had fallen. It had stopped raining though and I knew that I should leave. "Laura!" I called. No answer. "Laura!" Still no answer. I went back into the cave and back into the beautiful room but I stopped suddenly. Laura was gone and the room was just like the first room. Empty and ugly. I walked slowly out of the cave wondering what was going on. I stopped and saw the same deer I had seen before it started raining. Then I noticed something else. The deer had eyes just like Laura's. They were the same bright green! I slowly walked home. Would I ever see Laura again? Had I imagined the whole thing? I looked over my shoulder and saw the deer run gracefully into the woods.

Susan Shea/grade 5
Pullman Elementary School, St. Paul Park

MY WONDROUS FIND

I found a monster inside my china dog.
In the monster I found a battered old pipe.
In the old pipe I found some popcorn making a trail.
Following the trail, I found a piece of chalk.
In the white of the chalk, I found a flute
Blowing a beautiful orchestra song,
And inside the song
I found my china dog listening.

Lynne Zeige/grade 5
Murphy Elementary School, Grand Rapids

THE REFLECTION
(From a Painting by Magritte)

In his bathroom at 8:05
this man got up, and
    he
        was
            disappointed
because when he looked
in the mirror, his
            reflection
       was
backwards.
He got out his book of
phenomena. On page 111
it said, "no way to
cure, break your mirror."

Jeff Maas/grade 4
Edgewood Elementary School, Brooklyn Park

THE GIRLISH TREE

There was a girl who found two leaves and
came indoors holding them out saying to
her parents that she was a tree. As
winter came and the
girl was still hanging onto the leaves
her leaves turned red. The girl went
for walks and talked to the trees
while always holding onto the leaves.
Suddenly she grew older and with her
age she had gotten the longest legs and
arms. Her hair brushed out into
long strands. She drank
gallons of water in one gulp and
she grew even more. The girl could
see the whole town in a couple of
days. She aged and her branches
creaked as she watched people walk
right by. Nobody knew the tree.

Lisa Erickson/grade 12
Rush City High School, Rush City

Where is my secret?
I had a secret once, but I
lost it in the woods.
Did a bluebird take it, as I walked
down the path?
Or did the tree grab it
with his long branches like arms?
Did the wind blow
it to Oregon? Or did I lose
it in my heart?

Tony Thaler/ grade 4
Gideon Pond Elementary School, Burnsville

THE LANGUAGE OF LIGHT

Invented by the sun, who speaks
it with a powerful authority.
Taught to the light bulbs first,
who speak among themselves
of broken toasters, TV sets,
and lives of people. Awful gossips!
Taught the language to the stars
but left out words like "revolt"
and "competition" to guard her rights
and so they flicker with
uncertain light, like the fireflies
overheard—and picked up.
Taught fire how to glow so softly. . .
but fire is vain and tries to leap
about to win the friendship of
sparks, fireworks, whatever's
up to celebrating.
Taught the lesson too fast
for strobe lights to get it right
and now they copy it, frantically.
Failed to teach the moon,
mirrors, lakes. None could comprehend
so all they do is
echo what all the others say.

Kristin Maschka/grade 8
Mankato East Junior High, Mankato

COMPAS Writers & Artists-in-the-Schools is a program of COMPAS, the statewide community art agency. Through COMPAS Writers & Artists-in-the Schools, professional poets, fiction writers, playwrights, visual artists and musicians travel to Minnesota schools each year conducting residencies which are typically one week in length. During the 1982-83 school year 30,000 students in over 140 public and private schools worked directly with professional artists and learned from them the skills and techniques of particular disciplines.

At the completion of each school year representative student work from each writing residency is selected and gathered into an anthology of creative writing. *The Language of Light* is COMPAS' 1983 celebration of the skills, imagination and energy of students, teachers and artists in Minnesota. It is a tribute to the students who have dared to take artistic risks, to the teachers and administrators whose commitment to the best education possible brought artists into their schools, and, finally, a tribute to the artists whose expertise and generosity made possible these works of art. COMPAS acknowledges and thanks all those whose talents and enthusiasm have brought about *The Language of Light*.

Sheila Murphy, Director   David Mura, Associate Director
COMPAS Writers & Artists-in-the-Schools

Production of *The Language of Light* by Sheila Murphy and David Mura, assisted by Sharon Stein, Beth Lorentz, Susan Federbusch, June Lowe, Lennaea Luera, and Mary Burrell.

Index of Names

Susan Adams   123
Jennifer Anderson   32
Julie Athman   79
Sharon Bachman   145
Nina Barjesteh   93
Kathy Barrows   21
Jennifer Baltes   65
Liz Bamberg   165
Ann Bauer   91
Jenny Belisle   148
Brad Benike   139
Denise Berg   150
Becky Birch   35
Cameron Black   154
Russell Boebert   85
Andrew Bonnette   160
Andrea Bruchu   51
Melissa Buben   49
Sheri Byrne   59
Paul Christensen   152
John Cooper   124
Karen Cooper   84
Bob Daily   54
Kerry Dammen   125
Ryan Danielson   33
Scott Dolan   88
Dave Edinger   41
Maria Edington   96
Lisa Erickson   170
Andy Flint   71
Cindy Falley   94
Nicole Forde   34
Bobby Foster   98
Kari Frechette   116
Fred Fremgen   74
Dan Fritsche   68
Tom Gibbons   164
Robert Goldberg   70
Peggy Grant   102
Ken Gust   52
Kris Hansen   115
Julie Haar   25
Molly J. Harten   66

Julie Haurykiewicz   105
All Hegquist   127
Meri Herrman   23
Denise Holmes   82
Rich Holmes   61
Joseph Hsieh   161
Bobbie Jo Huss   69
Peter Jacobs   138
Greg Johnson   106
Shane Johnson   118
Christine Jones   22
Helena Kriel   119
Julie Krueger   109
Brent Kubat   59
Nick Kuklok   73
Tim Kurowski   60
Tim Lander   129
Becky Leder   135
Amy Lee   144
Aaron Leichter   90
Val Leske   157
Jeff Maas   169
Margaret Marrier   42
Stephen Marsh   114
Kristin Maschka   172
Bruce Messelt   24
Stuart Meyer   136
Amy Jo Millner   41
David Mills   47
Brian Mosbey   46
Michele Narlock   133
Scot Ninneman   92
David Nolby   36
Steve Ochry   76
Nathan O'Conner   75
Jeremy Olsen   107
Marcy Olson   163
Lisa Peterson   27
LeAnn Phipps   29
Su Price   92
Christine Ramaley   40
Robbie Reed   140
Rachel Reksten   99

175

Peggy Renneberg 62
Troy Renslow 141
Alisa Richetti 81
Steve Robberstad 29
Carrie Saba 155
Karen Schillewaert 103
Jodi Schmieg 149
Jennifer Schultz 48
Steve Schwanz 153
Brad Schwartz 87
Mary Sharratt 108
Susan Shea 166
Matt Shuey 153
Tracy Siegfried 104
Craig Solem 56
Josh Squires 158
Amy Stacy 28
Christine Strander 134
Tana Stromseth 100
Keiko Sugisaka 72
Jeannie Sullivan 162
Connie Sutherland 80
Bridget Swanson 30
Keith Swanson 32
Mark Swenson 146
Lara Tebelius 50
Tony Thaler 171
Caroline Thomson 78
Craig Uhl 147
Jeff Ukestad 98
Julie Vennewitz 122
Tami Volk 104
Michael Wackerfuss 26
Risa Weidman 53
Tracey White 64
Jenny Woods 58
Steve Worner 120
Jason Walton 156
Mikey Ysker 20
Jayme Zackman 55
Lynne Zeige 168

Index of Schools and Writers Who Participated in the 1982-83 Program

School	Community	Writer
Alice Smith Elementary	Hopkins	Deborah Keenan
Apple Valley High School	Apple Valley	Deborah Keenan
		Bob Kearney
Armstrong Elementary School	Cottage Grove	Bob Kearney
Bar-None School	Anoka	Michael Moos
Battle Lake High School	Battle Lake	Bob Kearney
Bayport Elementary School	Bayport	Natalie Goldberg
Belle Plaine Elementary	Belle Plaine	Roseann Lloyd
Bemidji High School	Bemidji	Patricia Weaver Francisco
Blake Middle School	Hopkins	John Fenn
Breck School	Minneapolis	Margot Fortunato Kriel
Breckenridge Elem./ Middle School	Breckenridge	Roseann Lloyd
Buffalo Lake Public School	Buffalo Lake	Richard Solly
Caledonia Elementary School	Caledonia	Patricia Weaver Francisco
Cedar Island Elementary	Maple Grove	Alvaro Cardona-Hine
Central Elementary School	Winona	Jill Breckenridge
Central High School/ East High School	Duluth	Marisha Chamberlain
Central Middle School	Columbia Heights	John Caddy
Central Middle School	Eden Prairie	Patricia Weaver Francisco
Central Park Elementary School	Roseville	Ruth Roston
Chaska Elementary School	Chaska	Alvaro Cardona-Hine
Chaska Middle School	Chaska	Michael Moos
Cohasset Elementary School	Cohasset	Bob Kearney
Columbia Heights Sr. High School	Columbia Heights	Michael Moos
Colvill & Jefferson Elementary Schools	Red Wing	Jill Breckenridge
Coon Rapids Jr. High School	Coon Rapids	Michael Dennis Browne
Cornelia Alternative School	Edina	Bill Holm
Delano Middle School	Delano	Nellie DeBruyn
Detroit Lakes Jr. High School	Detroit Lakes	Nellie DeBruyn

177

School	City	Poet
Dover-Eyota High School	Eyota	Caroline Marshall
Crestview Elementary School	Cottage Grove	Patricia Weaver Francisco
East High School/ Denfield High School	Duluth	Bob Kearney
East Jr. High School	Mankato	Caroline Marshall
Edgewood Elementary School	Brooklyn Park	Ruth Roston
Edison Elementary	Moorhead	Michael Moos
Epiphany Learning Center	Coon Rapids	John Minczeski
Fergus Falls Elementary School	Fergus Falls	Nancy Paddock
Fergus Falls Middle School	Fergus Falls	Bob Kearney
Fergus Falls Sr. High School	Fergus Falls	Terry Spohn
Forest Lake Elementary School	Grand Rapids	Sigrid Bergie
Franklin Middle School	Thief River Falls	John Minczeski
Fridley Jr. & Sr. High School	Fridley	Marisha Chamberlin
Garden City Elementary School	Brooklyn Center	Nancy Paddock
Gatewood Elementary School	Hopkins	Deborah Keenan
Gibbon Public School	Gibbon	Sigrid Bergie
Gideon Pond Elementary School	Burnsville	Deborah Keenan
Glen Lake Elementary School	Hopkins	Deborah Keenan
Goodview School	Winona	Jill Breckenridge
Grand Rapids Sr. High School	Grand Rapids	Richard Solly
Grandview Middle School	Mound	Richard Solly
Harding High School	St. Paul	Margot Fortunato Kriel
Hillside Elementary School	Cottage Grove	Candyce Clayton
Howard Lake/ Waverly High School	Howard Lake	Bob Kearney
Howe Elementary School	Minneapolis	Alvaro Cardona-Hine
Jefferson High School	Bloomington	Margot Fortunato Kriel
John F. Kennedy Elementary School	Hastings	Ruth Roston
John Glenn Jr. High School	Maplewood	John Caddy
Jordan Elementary School	Jordan	Marisha Chamberlain
Lakeaires Elementary School	White Bear Lake	Margot Fortunato Kriel
Long Prairie Public School	Long Prairie	John Caddy
Mankato West High School	Mankato	Bob Kearney
Mariner High School	White Bear Lake	Deborah Keenan
Meadowbrook Elementary School	Hopkins	Deborah Keenan

School	City	Author
McGregor High School	McGregor	John Caddy
Monticello High School	Monticello	John Minczeski
Montrose Elementary School	Montrose	Richard Solly
Murphy Elementary School	Grand Rapids	Marisha Chamberlain
Newport Elementary School	Newport	Terry Spohn
Oltman Jr. High School	St. Paul Park	Jill Breckenridge
Orono Sr. High School	Long Lake	David Mura
Park Sr. High School	Cottage Grove	Michael Dennis Browne, Margot Fortunato Kriel
Pine Hill Elementary School	Cottage Grove	Alvaro Cardona-Hine
Pine River High School	Pine River	Michael Moos
Pinewood Elementary School	Rochester	Natalie Goldberg
Plymouth Jr. High School	Plymouth	Richard Solly
Probstfield Elementary	Moorhead	John Caddy
Pullman Elementary School	St. Paul Park	Bob Kearney
Rahn Elementary School	Eagan	Patricia Weaver Francisco
Rice Elementary School	Rice	Sigrid Bergie
Roosevelt Elementary School	South St. Paul	Jill Breckenridge
Rosemount High School	Rosemount	Nancy Paddock
Riverside Elementary School	Moorhead	Mark Vinz
Riverview Elementary School	Grand Rapids	Sigrid Bergie
Rogers Elementary School	Rogers	Patricia Weaver Francisco
Royal Oaks Elementary School	Woodbury	Alvaro Cardona-Hine
Rush City High School	Rush City	Bill Holm
St. Bartholomew School	Wayzata	Bob Kearney
St. Columba School	St. Paul	Bill Holm
St. James School	St. Paul	John Minczeski
St. Mary of the Lake School	White Bear Lake	Patricia Weaver Francisco
St. Thomas Academy	St. Paul	Bob Kearney
Salem Hills Elementary School	Inver Grove Heights	Ruth Roston
Savage Elementary School	Burnsville	Deborah Keenan
Shakopee Jr. High School	Shakopee	Bill Holm
Sky Oaks Elementary School	Burnsville	Alvaro Cardona-Hine
Southwest Elementary School	Grand Rapids	Michael Moos
Sunny Hollow Elementary School	New Hope	Kate Green
Sunset Terrace Elementary School	Rochester	Deborah Keenan

School	City	Author
Swanville Elementary School	Swanville	Michael Moos
Tanglen Elementary School	Hopkins	Deborah Keenan
Tilden Elementary School	Hastings	Alvaro Cardona-Hine
Valley View Jr. High School	Edina	Marisha Chamberlain
Warba Elementary School	Warba	Nellie DeBruyn
Washington Elementary School	Detroit Lakes	Sigrid Bergie
Washington Elementary School	Moorhead	Mark Vinz
Washington Elementary School	Rochester	Nancy Paddock
Washington Elementary School	South St. Paul	Richard Solly
West Elementary School	Worthington	John Minczeski
Westwood Elementary School	Blaine	Marisha Chamberlain
White Bear Sr. High School	White Bear Lake	Alvaro Cardona-Hine
William Byrne Elementary School	Burnsville	Richard Solly
Willmar Sr. High School	Willmar	Patricia Weaver Francisco
Wilshire Park Elementary School	Minneapolis	Roseann Lloyd
Wilson Elementary School	Owatonna	Natalie Goldberg
Woodbury Elementary School	Woodbury	Michael Dennis Browne
Woodbury Jr. High School	Woodbury	Michael Moos
Woodbury Sr. High School	Woodbury	Jill Breckenridge
Worthington Jr. High School	Worthington	Bob Kearney
Wyoming Elementary School	Wyoming	Michael Moos